St Ursula's in Danger

By the same author

Schoolgirl Chums

St Ursula's in Danger

Peter Glidewell

DRAGON
Granada Publishing

Dragon Books
Granada Publishing Ltd.
8 Grafton Street, London W1X 3LA

Published by Dragon Books 1983

British Library Cataloguing in Publication Data
Glidewell, Peter
St Ursula's in danger.—(St Ursula's)
I. Title II. Series
823'.914 [J] PZ7

ISBN 0-583-30684-5

Reproduced, printed and bound in Great Britain by
Hazell Watson & Viney Limited,
Member of the BPCC Group,
Aylesbury, Bucks

Set in Plantin

She looked towards the battlements
And there she did descry
A phantom on the old school roof
And a black cloud in the sky.

CHAPTER 1

A single blackbird sang lustily in its accustomed place outside the Remove wing at St Ursula's school for girls. It was a persistently cheerful bird and the song was penetrating. It told of territory . . . of mating time and the freshness of the new spring grass.

But today the blackbird had competition. For the window of number two study was thrown open to the April breeze. And from that open and leaded casement came another, louder, and in the blackbird's opinion very much inferior, sort of song.

'Oh, won't you stay to tea?' carolled the voice of Mr Al Bowley, echoing the latest number from the Lyceum Ballroom.

The clink of crockery too could be heard, and the answering hum of girlish voices, one of which belonged to none other than our old friend, Alison Dayne. Over a year had passed since that terrifying episode with the fire. It was a very different Alison indeed who now deposited a large plum cake in the very centre of the clean table cloth and then stood back to admire it.

'Looks good, don't you think?' she announced cheerfully to anyone who might be listening.

'Mm,' agreed a sticky voice from beside the mantelpiece. The speaker was a pretty, fair girl, with a snub nose set in an elfin face. The reason her voice was sticky was that her mouth was full of jam. And since they were at that moment in the act of scooping jam almost from the bottom of the pot, her fingers, too, were sticky. 'He should really enjoy it,' she said, trying to lick the drop of jam from the end of her nose. She replaced the pot amongst its fellows on the mantelpiece. 'It should really appeal.'

That the cake should not fail to please was as important to this latest addition to their study as it was to Alison herself. For the expected male visitor was none other than the amazing Edward Dayne, Alison's nineteen year old cousin and a once seen, never to be forgotten source of interest to the jam covered sylph of the Remove.

Alison knew it was only a fashion fad, but how ridiculously like their other two friends this Sally had managed to look. Except that Jen had grown apace, and that Hilary, the fourth member of the study, had gone to Africa for a spell, with her father the Bishop to show the poor heathens how ensnared and deluded they'd been for the last two hundred thousand years.

A spot of big game hunting was what Hilary would really have preferred, but as she had remarked sadly, there'd be little chance of *that*. In her imagination Hilary saw herself stalking big game in the hot, tawny grass, and triumphantly bringing back tiger skins and rhino horns to hang in their school study. But in more practical moments she knew the animals would be left in peace. Sitting about bored to death in pith helmet and white dress – the envy of the wives of the various chiefs who would be planning to copy her attire – was a more likely scene. Thoughts of hunters' spoil decorating the walls of the study had, therefore, to be abandoned.

Instead, they were all looking forward to a few native spears and the odd shrunken head to augment the present rather sparse collection of water colours of famous cities and the portrait of a Bosnavian nobleman by an unknown artist that at present adorned those rather bare walls. In fact, thought Alison, casting an anxious eye around, the room had a decidedly bleak look. Still, there was a splendid fire in a brass grate, just right for toasting crumpets. And somehow the Victorian Tudor wooden surround contrived to look even more Tudor than the real thing.

The door burst open and Jennifer flew in.

'Alison . . . Oh, I say. Expecting company?'

'Only Teddy,' Alison laughed.

'*Only*, she says!' Sally choked over an Eccles cake. 'What it must be like to be able to feel so casual!'

'He's quite an ordinary chap,' Alison fibbed.

'Not half decent though . . . and as for that dreamy bike . . .'

'Oh, ho! Now we're getting nearer the mark,' giggled Alison hopefully.

'Pooh. Fudge!'

'Well anyway,' Jennifer announced, flinging her arms along the back of the sofa as she plonked down . . . 'Sorry to be a beastly bore, but Kitty was missing from roll call again. Peggy said to tell you.'

'Oh? Really?'

Lines appeared on that fair brow. They were lines that had come too often of late, and threatened permanent imprint. Since the arrival a few weeks ago of Teddy's little sister, life at St Ursula's had become unpleasantly complicated for Alison Dayne, who now found herself almost snapping: 'And what does she expect *me* to do about it?'

'Well . . . find her old thing, of course. That's about the long and short of it,' Jennifer yawned. Since Hilary's departure, the girl had taken on her friend's role as leader of the Remove, and in her manner there was a dangling sarcasm that had Alison rising instantly.

'I thought discipline was the prefects' job?'

'Discipline? What discipline?' Jennifer's howl of derision sounded like water gurgling down a sink. 'Since dear, darling Miss Devine hopped off to Bosnavia I should say discipline's a thing of the past my pet – or hadn't you noticed?'

Jumping up and grabbing the tin, she began to search for biscuits, arranging them along the back of her hand and choosing the one with the cherry.

'It's all right,' said Sally tersely. 'You won't be needing those.'

'Won't I?' Jennifer blinked in surprise. With a meaningful

look, the other girl suddenly swept away the biscuits and replaced them in the cupboard.

'Oh! I see!' Jennifer sprang up. In the space of that few minutes, the whole atmosphere in number two study had changed subtly and unaccountably. It had altered very much for the worse. Sally was glaring at Jennifer. Jennifer was glowering at Sally in a way that made that young madam bite her lip. 'Want to get rid of me eh?'

'Oh, *bother* Kitty,' Alison moaned, too busy with her own problem to care about anyone else's. 'I suppose I'll have to go, just when everything's ready. That child's going to play the giddy goat once too often . . .'

Grabbing a mac, she left the room. Sally's anxious voice came floating after her down the passage—

'I say . . . Ali? D'you think he'd give me a pillion ride actually, that adorable cousin of yours?'

'Might do,' came back the acid reply. 'Depends how much you suck up to him.'

And now she was on her bicycle pedalling furiously and feeling as savage as a moment ago she'd been blithe. If losing Hilary had been tragic, at this moment gaining Kitty appeared far worse. She'd really been looking forward to having Teddy to tea for the first time ever and showing off her study to this lofty and adored cousin. Whether or not Teddy realized the fact, the responsibility for making up for Hilary's absence had been dumped fairly and squarely on his ample masculine shoulders. Now, once again, Kitty was spoiling everything. She knew where the child had gone, of course. It was simply where everyone seemed to be going that term – the current fad.

'One of *the* Forsons my dear – the Parkinson Forsons no less.'

'Who?'

'Don't they teach anything in schools these days?' sarcastic fathers had asked dryly in the face of such flagrant dimness.

For Mr Forson was an oil king, one of the richest men in the world.

The arrival on their doorstep of such a 'name' had aroused the keenest speculation amongst the girls at St Ursula's. And when he'd thrown open his grounds for their use with such magnanimity, the response had been eager and uncontrolled. Discipline had *indeed* been lax that term; the prefects, after Miss Devine's departure, were left very much in control. And since the American possessed both badminton and tennis courts . . . surely he was a good thing. Which was why, at four thirty on this rather chilly April afternoon, Alison found herself on her bicycle turning in at the imposing gates of Coxley Grange.

First along the drive she passed the surly looking gardener who straightened as she went by, then tilted back his moth eaten hat to watch her go. Convinced as she was that she had not misjudged the man's character, Alison wasted no time exchanging pleasantries. Next, she found herself shuddering as she came to the repellent line of dead birds and rodents that hung outside a jauntily painted gypsy caravan, poked into a space among the trees.

Its occupant with, as usual, only his head visible over the bottom half of the door, caused her no wasted time either. Some people at school swore he was a dwarf, deposited there by a passing flea circus. Alison, on the other hand, tended to think him merely a lazy good for nothing who sat on his bottom by day, and only emerged at night . . . to poach.

Last, but by no means least, on a dreary corner of the lake, there was the 'encampment'. It had been built by the rougher elements of the village, boys it was said – again there were conflicting opinions at St Ursula's. Kinder souls claimed it was a hide, built expressly to watch birds. Cynics guessed it was rather to shoot them – particularly the poor mallards who in his lordship's day had had the place to themselves. Whatever its purpose, the canvas covered tree platform was an eyesore and not at all what you'd expect in such resplendent grounds.

Evidently a Democrat by persuasion, the American certainly seemed determined to live up to his ideals. And as Alison scrunched to a halt under the white statue of Venus that surmounted the entrance to that imposing mansion, she wondered again at the peculiar magnanimity of the man, for the door at the top of the steps was, as usual, open.

Without knocking, she ventured to enter. She could hear Kitty's clear, impatient voice. In the familiar and ingenuous tones she habitually used to charm and seduce, the child was arguing.

'But I still don't see why you should have gotten yourself into such a state, little 'un,' came the reply to whatever it was she'd just said. 'I mean, I've always thought St Ursula's was a real *nice* school . . . and that things for you were kinda . . . well . . . hot dickety? They haven't been bullying you, have they?'

'Oh no, Mr Forson . . . nothing like that. It's just that I don't want to stay there any more.'

Alison crossed the marble floor of the bust lined hall. Then, pausing a moment, she tapped on the door of the room from which the voices emanated. Unlike Kitty, she'd never been in the house before, and also unlike Kitty she found its opulence a trifle overpowering. Mr Forson looked up as she came hesitantly in. Cigar puffing and intense conversation both halted in mid breath.

The thickset American radiated the rubicund cheerfulness of an English country gentleman. The cheeky check suited figure and the wide smile gave out unwavering warmth and confidence. His trim moustache made him look like everyone's Daddy. Perhaps, thought Alison, critically comparing him with her own father, the white shirt was just a little too white, the bow tie a little too red. The hanky in the top pocket was simply too flamboyant altogether. But these were trivia, and Alison, like everyone else, found herself crumbling instantly before the easy, unaffected charm of the man.

'Sorry to bother you – the door was open so I came in.'

'No problem, my dear.'

His arms waved expansively to include the whole study and Mrs Forson too, sitting quietly embroidering under the plaque of the American Eagle. She looked the glamorous epitomy of a president's wife. There was no sign of Kitty.

'You must be *Alison* Dayne?' beamed Mr Forson.

'Yes.'

The slumped figure, squatting hopefully out of sight behind the high back of the leather sofa, could no longer escape.

'I'm not coming!'

'You've got to, Kitty. There'll be no end of a row if you don't.'

Alison was only too aware of what that row might mean. With Miss Devine away, the prefects tended to act first and think afterwards, if they thought at all.

'I'm not,' Kitty assured her, and the child's voice sounded unusually stubborn. 'I saw something very creepy on the landing in school. I looked for you but you had gone to the shop.'

'Gee,' said the American without any hesitation. 'A phantom.'

'What's that?' Kitty enquired sulkily. Alison felt in no mood to explain.

'Kitty ... if you're making this up to get out of something ...'

The nine year old vehemently shook her head.

'I *did* see her, honestly Alison. A silvery grey lady, up where we go to bed.'

Alison sighed. Whatever would the little pest think of next?

'I guess she means it,' the American declared in reverent tone, and Alison could cheerfully have strangled him.

'Please don't make me come back,' Kitty pleaded. 'She might be there again.'

The fear in the blue eyes was only too evident, and at this quite unexpected turn of events Alison found herself biting her lip in perplexity. Was it possible? She had to think of something, and think quickly.

'I'm sure she won't,' she began, and paused for a moment. 'I could try and get you in our dorm for the night.'

The child brightened and went immediately across to her cousin.

'Gosh . . . yes!'

'Thank you Mrs Forson, for looking after her.'

'A pleasure, I'm sure.'

As the two girls turned to leave the room, Mr Forson seemed to stir himself from his reverie.

'Gee. A real English phantom!' he murmured in wistful tones, adding: 'Now you just don't think any more about it, Kitty honey. And then in a few days' time it'll all seem like a bad dream . . . won't it?'

He led the way out, rolling affably over the marble slabs and towards that ever open front entrance which only a moment ago the butler had closed. A faintly threatening breeze had come up suddenly, disturbing the tapestries and blowing magazines open on the big table in the corner. As the door opened, Kitty gave a little scream. From the top step, a sinister person was peering at them, apparently with some difficulty. But as the queer figure in the long leather coat removed the scarf from its mouth and then its goggles, both girls cried out gleefully: 'Teddy!'

'Ah ha. Your friend Sally said I might find you here.'

'Surely she didn't chase you away?'

'No – on the contrary. That's partly why I'm here. You know shy little me. Actually, I thought I'd give the kid a lift on the Thunderer.'

The boy glanced fondly towards his latest motor bike where it stood beside Alison's less glamorous machine.

'Say,' cried Forson, 'aren't we going to be introdooced?'

'Oh golly yes,' said Alison, going a little pink. 'Mr Forson, this is my cousin – Kitty's big brother.'

'Hi! Glad to make your acquaintance.' The American stuck out a hand, which was firmly grasped in return. 'My oh my, but that's some machine you've got there.'

'Ten fine horses . . .'

'Well, just you two be careful on that thing.'

'Thanks ever so much for being so nice to me, Mr Forson.' Kitty flashed her most winning smile.

'That's all right, sweetie.'

The bluff American smiled and tickled his small protegée under the chin. Then wandering after them he rammed the cigar back in his mouth and watched them depart. The big machine rolled gently over the gravel and Kitty turned back for a final wave. But Mr Forson had already gone.

'Well!' gasped Sally, toasting her fingers as well as the crumpet for a moment as the three burst in, 'a drove of Daynes at last. I thought you'd *never* come.' She rose, and with a generous wave of the hand indicated a table covered with good things to eat. Teddy, languidly pulling off his big gloves, looked around him with appreciation.

'Some spread!'

'I say,' Kitty squeaked, 'crumpets! I love crumpets.'

Alison laughed shakily.

'Of all the good, thoughtful creatures, Sally.'

'I borrowed the odd meringue. We Spencers know our place. The last resort of the poor and proud.'

'Oh fiddlesticks.'

'Can I have one now?' piped a small voice.

'You, my girl,' replied Alison sternly, 'are going down to tea like all the others.'

By all the 'others' she meant, of course, all those junior brats amongst whom she herself had been numbered until a term ago. Family favouritism was a thing not to be encouraged at St Ursula's. Kitty responded with a winning pout at her big brother and an 'Oh, *Alison!* How can you be so beastly?' – but it was no good appealing to either of them, it seemed.

'So absolutely howwid,' Teddy mimicked as he flopped gratefully down on to the somewhat tattered sofa. 'Off you go, young 'un. Do as your guardian angel says.'

'I can come to your dorm though?' Kitty spoke anxiously.

'I'll have to ask Miss Cowley.'

'Oh *she* won't mind,' pronounced the urchin, now with complete confidence. 'Thanks, Ali.'

As the child departed Sally asked, 'What's up with her?' in a puzzled voice.

'She's been having nightmares again. Where's Jen, by the bye?'

Sally's cheeks tinged with colour. She cleared her throat.

'I sent her away. Teddy, can I butter you something?' she enquired quickly.

Beneath those fluttering eyelids, a winning smile had been switched on and was now being flashed at the visitor.

'It's all right. I can do it.'

'No, no,' Sally insisted, '*do* let me.'

Goodness, Alison thought, girls could be syrupy at times.

'All right, fine.'

Leaning back, hands behind his head, Teddy seemed loftily amused by all the female attention.

'Cosy little den you have here,' he remarked. 'Better than my study was, even in the sixth.'

Sally responded with a click of the tongue. 'Boys don't know how to look after themselves half the time.' She buttered then handed over his crumpet. 'Jam? We've got four sorts: plum, gooseberry, loganberry, quince . . .'

'Plum, please.'

Sally, flipping her fingers along the jars on the mantelpiece, gave a disappointed frown.

'Bother! The jar's nearly empty.'

'Yes,' Alison cheerfully agreed as she bit into the hot oozing crispness of one of those buttered delicacies. 'I wonder why?'

'No cause for alarm. I'll toddle next door again.'

'I'll have quince,' Teddy shouted after the girl, whose face immediately came popping back round the door.

'Good heavens, Teddy, it's no *trouble*,' she dimpled.

This was a *little* excessive, even for such a hardened man of the world. Edward Dayne took the opportunity of pulling his favourite cousin protectively down on to the floor beside him. As for Alison, she allowed herself to lean upon that well built frame, with a sigh of pleasure at last.

A certain loneliness had lately crept unobserved into the girl's life, and having Teddy just down the road in Stalminster made all the difference.

'I *am* sorry about Kitty,' the boy apologized frankly. 'What's she been up to otherwise?'

'Well,' giggled Alison, 'Claudia Hiram murdered her rabbit.'

'Claudia Hiram?'

'Yes, her best friend. She pulled its ears off.'

'Not very friendly. Was the animal wild?'

'No – woollen! It didn't feel a thing.'

'How about Claudia Hiram?'

Alison laughed delightedly. This sort of banter had been going on since they'd been children and it came as quite a shock to find Sally once more back in their midst.

'*Aren't* we the cosy little couple?'

Was there a tinge of bitterness in the voice? It disappeared anyway as the girl plonked the results of her expedition down on the table.

'I hunted *everywhere*,' she gasped. 'This is Biddy Barton's granny's special Victoria – or so it says on the label. And now,' she breathed, sinking in a theatrical heap and leaning, chin on hand, upon the back of the easy chair, 'you've got to tell me just *all* about it.'

Teddy blinked. 'All about what?'

'Why,' Sally giggled as she bit her bottom lip, 'that incredible bike, of course.'

CHAPTER 2

Two hours had passed. It was now seven o'clock. Visitors were allowed at St Ursula's on Sunday afternoons and had normally to be off the premises by six. But with neither Miss Devine nor even Miss Prosser to hustle away anxious parents, there seemed less and less point to such rules.

At last, with a glance at his watch, Teddy sprang to his feet crying, 'Gad! I'd better be going. I've got a whole lot of stuff to get ready for tomorrow.'

As well as being articled to a local solicitor, the boy was studying as conscientiously as he could for his legal exams. No genius, he was no slacker either. He would gain that place in his father's firm if it killed him; which, judging from his build, it appeared unlikely to do. When Edward Dayne got his teeth into something, he tended to stick to it. Now he and his cousin were walking together down the gloomy passage towards the main staircase.

'Nice kid actually, that Sally,' he reflected, frowning, as though only now he was having to leave her had the other girl's existence finally penetrated his consciousness. 'Didn't her brother play rugger at one time?'

These were serious words. If Teddy mentioned rugger, it meant more than a passing interest. In spite of herself, Alison could not help feeling piqued. Normally Alison would not have thought hers was a jealous nature. It came, therefore, as a surprise to her to hear her own voice reply with such anxiety:

'Not for the *County* like you though, Teds. I'm glad you're living so close by.' She slipped a proprietorial arm through his. 'It isn't just Daddy I've missed.'

The boy gave the arm an affectionate squeeze.

'Boarding schools can be queer places. I only hope Kitty settles down. I'm supposed to be keeping an eye on the little pest.'

Alison nodded. They were approaching the landing at the head of the solid oak staircase that led to the juniors' dormitories. If she clutched her cousin more tightly, it was not simply out of family feeling. No. There was something different and decidedly suspect about the old school tonight. As if he sensed it too, Teddy paused and looked enquiringly at his companion. Alison answered his unspoken question.

'Yes. This is the place.'

The draught under the adjacent door blew strongly enough to make a sharp little moan. Even the best scrum half the County had had in three years was felt to stiffen slightly.

'Listen,' he muttered.

'What? What is it? I can't hear anything.'

'That wind. Otherwise, it's so darned quiet. A grey lady . . . It isn't really like Kitty to tell lies.'

'Just stories.'

Looking down at Alison, Teddy cleared his throat. Then he forced a laugh.

'Remember how *you* used to see things?'

'*Me*?'

'Yes. When you lived over at the Vicarage. I can see your dad never pressed the point. You just used to smile and stare at something no-one else could see.'

'How d'you know this?'

'I witnessed it, dear cous. I was actually present. You were about two years old at the time and I was six, and you put the fear of Old Nick into me – standing there smiling and then walking towards an invisible something, holding out your hands.'

'Good Lord!'

'I suppose I shouldn't have brought the matter up.'

'The Daynes are like that,' said Alison quietly.

'Oh come on,' Teddy blinked uneasily. 'You're getting *me* jumpy now. Maybe she just spotted that picture.'

He peered at the portrait, cracked and dirty with age. Underneath the grime the outlines of the gracious Elizabethan lady were so faded by time and obscured by dust as to be virtually indistinguishable. Alison gave the painted necklace round the lady's throat a perfunctory wipe.

'Mmm,' she observed ruefully, 'like everything else round here, it needs a good clean. The whole place has gone to pot since Miss Cowley came.' She flopped down the stairs, one by one; and Teddy followed.

'Seems pretty easy going I must say, your new Head. Doesn't object to me being here, for instance?'

'Absolutely not. In a moment I'll go in there and ask about Kitty coming up, and she won't mind that either.'

'Seems ironic, I must say.'

They had arrived at the bottom of the stairs.

'What seems ironic?'

'Well, this Cowley. I thought your father sent you to St Ursula's because of someone called Miss Devine? Weren't they planning to get married at one time?'

'They certainly were not! And anyway, he now claims there was another reason altogether.'

'What other reason?'

'Something for him to know, and me to find out.'

'*Eh*?'

'He wouldn't say,' Alison explained patiently. 'Claimed it might spoil my relationship with the other girls.'

'Good Lord.' Teddy scratched his head in perplexity. 'Dark horse, your dad, what?'

When he happened to glance at the door by which they were standing, the boy nearly jumped back up the stairs.

'Golly! I didn't know we were standing right next to the old dame's hidey hole.' Although Miss Devine's study, the name firmly inscribed on the panelling was now 'Margaret Cowley'. Teddy was not accustomed to lowering his voice, but he actually whispered now. '*That* looks pretty permanent, I must say!'

'I assure you it isn't. She's quite pathetically temporary.'

'Nevertheless . . . shouldn't we be wandering along?'

'If you like.'

'I mean, supposing she's heard us?'

'She won't have. She's not the listening type. And she usually lies with a cushion on her head about this time in the evening. Really. I like her. I can't help it. Sally dismisses her in two words flat. She says she's cracked. It *is* odd Miss Devine choosing such a queer stand in; but then, that's Miss Devine all over.'

'Act of charity, you mean? Felt sorry for the old fruit?' Teddy sounded frankly disbelieving. 'Still, frightfully convenient for everyone, I should say.'

They had now wandered through the main entrance and out into the open air. Stars had appeared in a pale sky. For the umpteenth time already that term, Alison found herself perplexed.

'I know what you mean,' she replied with a shiver. 'The poor lamb can't help it, I s'pose, but school shouldn't *be* like that. Miss Cowley can just about cope with the upper third, but when it comes to Kitty Dayne and the rest of those first year imps – well!'

Alison shrugged, and then raised her hands to the heavens.

For Kitty, as for most other schoolgirls, the first lesson on a Monday morning was apt to be a time of pain and torment. Nevertheless, with the rest of the first form at St Ursula's School for Girls, she had recently been discovering ways of relieving this tedium. The arrival a fortnight ago of the 'acting' (for Miss Cowley was nothing if not entertaining) Headmistress, had already brought a new and welcome dimension to the study of the English language.

Even at this moment, Kitty sat breathless with excitement as the temporary teacher prepared to play for the fourth time her heavy piano chord. It was one way of achieving silence without even speaking, let alone shouting. Miss Cowley's lungs had never been good. She had spent too much time in damp beds up and down the country as she travelled from school to school ever to get rid of that slightly husky tone which told of a perpetual sore throat.

In some schools, she had even known the piano chord method to work. Whatever the case, it was always worth a try, particularly if there were a piano in the room, and anyway, *she* was soothed by the melodious sounds, even if the girls weren't. She'd have played a whole tune if she'd been able. Somehow, the ability to capitalize on that first rosy flush of inspiration and continue right through to the end had always eluded her. She supposed it needed concentration, a quality she was the first to admit she singularly lacked.

Used to embracing anything from algebra to domestic

science – whatever happened to be needed at the time – her pupils had been older girls in the main, often quite interested in their subject and frequently more able to teach her than she them. Indeed, never before had Miss Cowley held responsibility for a whole school, from the top to this – the very distressing bottom – because never before had she been a Headmistress, even a temporary one. For years she'd been fitting in here, and filling in there.

When Miss Devine, daughter of her old college friend Marcia Devine, had so surprisingly offered her charge of St Ursula's, as big and important a school as any in the country, the chance had come as a welcome uplift, sorely needed at a period of financial strain. Miss Cowley had in fact been seriously thinking of giving up school life altogether and retiring with her sister to the fruit farm in Kent. The idea of picking apples in the total peace of the countryside (for in 1933 there were few cars and virtually no aeroplanes) held a compelling appeal for a person whose ears rang with the din of thirty years of clamour. So soothed was she by that fourth chord, that she was just contemplating another when, with a tremendous crash, the lid of the fine grand piano slammed down. The mistress sprang into the air with a shriek.

'Who did that?'

The whole form rose as a silent body. Breathing heavily, nerves shattered, the mistress pursed her lips and, stroking the veins that ran along them, gazed at the backs of her hands. Patiently, carefully, she allowed her shock to subside. Really, they were fine hands, suited to something better than wielding chalk. They were pianist's hands; she had decided it long ago.

She came out of her little dream with a sigh and, glancing up at the eager waiting faces, murmured absently, 'Very well. You will take fifty lines.'

'All of us Miss Cowley?'

'Yes. All of you.'

'That's two lines each, isn't it?'

'I suppose so. Now. *Richard the Second.*'

The name slipped easily from the tongue because it was one of the only two Shakespeare epics she knew. Sometimes Miss Cowley wondered if there had ever been a First. If so, she was sure he must have been a fine man, unlike this weedy, verbose specimen. Richard the First! She almost found herself murmuring the magic name aloud but, as sooner or later they could invariably be relied upon to do, a child interrupted her just in time.

'Oh no, Miss Cowley.'

'What dear?'

'Not *Richard the Second*. It's *The Tempest* this term.'

'I stand corrected.' What a blessed relief! She could relax – expand even. For this was her 'other' work; indeed, her favourite of all two plays. It was a poem, a mercy of escapism with which she was almost entirely familiar. A smile at last played about the mistress's lips.

'A play of storms at sea,' she exulted, clasping her hands together, 'of shipwrecked sailors and a mighty sorcerer.'

And she swivelled to the blackboard with a flourish that almost had her spinning from the platform. For the hem of her long dress had again caught in the heel that was coming off her shoe. It took a few jerking movements to unsteadily regain her balance and reach for the chalk. One always reached for chalk – if only to prove one could write. But when Miss Cowley did so, the substance quite often had an elusive quality; either it was lost, or hidden by some child seeking vulgar amusement. This time it slid.

She could see it now, actually sliding, drawn by a long piece of cotton thread down that narrow, dusty channel at the base of the blackboard, just as her fingers were about to close over the substance. What *were* the dratted creatures called that a hundred biology lessons had told her had slaved over making the wretched stuff in the first place? It was just this kind of useless information that always stuck in the mind. Try remembering the date of the French Revolution! Globigerina and Textu something – yes, Textularia! That was their stupid name. Well, confound the little pests for having done their work so assiduously! They could have saved themselves the trouble as far as she was concerned. With a clear little crack the white stick composed, apparently, entirely of tiny sea shells, fell to the floor and snapped. Miss Cowley snapped too, driven to reaction in spite of her training.

'You all did that as well, I suppose?'

'Yes, Miss Cowley. Sorry, Miss Cowley.'

'Then you will all replace it.'

There came a dash for the chalk as, led by that one curly-haired imp she must really keep her eye on, the whole form rushed to obey. And Miss Cowley knew that she must surely be losing her grip to have made such a foolish suggestion. Wincing, she picked up her book.

'Thankfully,' she announced, as the wretches returned to their seats at last, 'this is one of Shakespeare's more cheerful plays, set on a desert island somewhere near . . .'

'Italy?' squeaked someone.

'Correct, child. What is your name?'

'Nesta Roberts.'

'Then, Nesta, remind me to give you a part in our reading this morning.'

'Oh, if only we could perform it properly – at Coxley's, I mean, beside the lake – and the whole school attend!'

As Nesta clasped her hands, her voice had enlarged with possibility and romance.

'Ooh, yes!' This was that curly-haired one suddenly piping up again, her voice rising above the babble of the others. 'And I could be Ariel, flitting through the trees like a little bee. I've got the wings – yellow ones. I had them at my last school.'

Miss Cowley found herself frowning. There was trickery in the air. She suddenly felt very bad tempered indeed. Something had been nagging at her ever since her arrival at this school, and now she remembered what it was.

'Why must you do everything at this Coxley Grange?' she enquired irritably, smoothing back her waves of ginger hair. 'I'm tired of watching the whole junior school traipsing across to that American's house. What is wrong with performing the play in our own grounds, if it *has* to be outside at this uncertain time of year?'

'But Miss Cowley,' Nesta objected succinctly, 'that wouldn't be the same at all. There's no island or lake or anything.'

'No,' decided the mistress with sudden unexpected firmness, 'I am going to put my foot down. I'd like you to stop going to Mr Forson's altogether.'

'You can't *do* that!' a horrified Philippa Treadway shrieked. 'You *can't* stop us, when Major Farquhar specifically said we could. He's the Chairman of the Governors . . .'

Although these children had not the least idea of what a Governor's function might be, they evidently knew that the seedy looking, blue faced Farquhar was a person of considerable influence. Since Miss Devine's departure, indeed, this old military man seemed an ever present force, continually hovering about the building, taking every opportunity to interfere with the smooth running of the establishment. For her part, Miss Cowley had already seen quite enough of the ex-Whitehall civil servant. Frankly, she regarded him as a slightly ridiculous old porpoise, frequently surfacing to blow out air. The way the man went on, anyone would think she didn't know her job, and she therefore responded hotly:

'It seems to me that Major Farquhar is forever meddling in matters that do not concern him.'

'Oh, no,' contradicted Nesta Roberts with infuriating self-assurance. '*He's* the one who decides things while Miss Devine's away, and he said if we were good . . .'

'You are *not* good.'

There was such a clamour that the poor lady was forced to insert a finger in each ear.

'We are when we're there, Miss Cowley!'

'It's only a craze, Miss Cowley.'

'Mr Forson's *so* nice to us.'

'He gives us sweets.'

'We have fun in the shubbery and climb trees.'

'He's so kind. He lets in all the village children. There are some awfully nice boys who've built a splendid camp. They know exactly where all the best nests are.'

'Good gracious! These are no reasons whatever.'

'But Miss Cowley,' Philippa interrupted, 'Mr Forson is most fearfully rich. After Miss Devine left for Bosnavia, Nesta heard him telling the Major he would build us a new swimming pool – if we were nice to him.'

'*Nice* to him?' Good Heavens. What did that mean? Miss Cowley passed a hand over her fevered brow. She had evidently allowed the matter to get quite out of hand. All that was to be hoped was that she could remedy this laxness before something awful occurred. *If*, indeed, she was not already too late.

'Yes, nice to him. Don't you know what that means? It means cheer him up 'cos he's lonely here without anybody not stuck up to talk to. We've got to go there and be jolly nice: we've just *got* to!'

'I remain quite unimpressed by any of this. I shall go to Mr Forson and make my feelings known to him this very afternoon.' In the class, pandemonium now ensued. Visibly trembling, the mistress shrieked: 'If you do not restore order, I shall punish you severely.'

No-one took any notice.

'It's not fair,' came the enraged replies. 'It's what we like best of all.'

'Very well,' Miss Cowley suddenly yelled above the din. 'I warned you.'

There was a tall, narrow cupboard in the corner of the classroom, always referred to, for some reason lost in the mists of time, as the 'map' cupboard. Towards this the harassed female now started and, after a last shuddering look around, disappeared inside. The door closed. Miss Cowley was no longer in their midst. The girls, no longer capable of surprise at anything their acting Head did, continued to hurl their grievances at the cupboard door.

'You never said anything to Kitty Dayne about not being in to roll call yesterday,' shouted Claudia Hiram angrily, eyeing her best friend with a mixture of distrust and loathing. 'She didn't even come to bed last night.'

'There was a *cause*,' came a muffled voice from the cupboard.

'How long are you staying in the cupboard, Miss Cowley?'

'I said I would punish you. I am now punishing you severely,' came the reply, 'and I'm not coming out until complete order is restored.'

'I slept with Alison in her bed.' Kitty spoke complacently, ignoring entirely the above remarks. '*And* I'm being allowed to go there again tonight.'

'You're a hateful pig, Kitty,' Claudia burst out in an agony of distraction and envy. 'Just because you've got a cousin in the school.'

'It is *not* because she's got a cousin in the school,' came the voice from the cupboard.

'Then what is it?'

'If you must know,' declared Kitty importantly, 'it's because I saw a phantom.'

Total silence fell upon the class.

Before we go any further, one thing ought to be made quite clear. This word 'phantom' was a very recent addition to Kitty's vocabulary, and she hadn't much idea of its precise meaning. (She remembered Mr Forson using it and suggesting that the grey lady might be one.) Perhaps the grey lady was just somebody's visiting mother. Some children did have the most interesting mothers, and Kitty had often envied them. But it was odd the way she seemed to disappear through the wall so suddenly – one moment there, the next not there. Probably the rustling person had simply gone somehow through the door into the dormitory when she wasn't looking properly. But Kitty wasn't going to tell the form that. No, she was going to make as much of the story as she possibly could. She got little enough attention round here, and there was nothing like a good story to get people going in a school.

Indeed before she'd come to St Ursula's, Kitty had successfully managed to get one Headmistress in England to phone the police with a rumour about an escaped grizzly bear. Alison's small cousin was not an actual liar. She had seen that bear. The fact that it turned out later to be just an old English sheepdog digging up a very smelly dead rabbit was the least interesting aspect. What *had* been curious was the sense of panic the affair produced in the school, with girls screaming about going to bed, and girls asking her to describe the bear again and again – just what colour of fur it had, and what its teeth were like and then, when she told them, asking her to stop. Yes, it had really been most satisfying. You couldn't keep *on* doing it, of course, but she was fairly new at St Ursula's and a teenyweeny bit of exaggeration gave a person a certain importance.

She had not, as yet, made her mark in the school. With that vague but worrying sense of opportunities missed, Kitty now felt no compunction about laying it on really thick. The form's reaction was most satisfyingly enthusiastic – hysterical, even.

'A phantom?' they cried, dismayed. 'What sort of phantom, for goodness sake?'

Kitty licked her lips. A shadow of a smile played over them, all her fear of the horrid thing forgotten in the glory of the moment.

'A tall grey lady,' she announced, glancing at Claudia to see how her friend in particular would take the news. 'Very pale and beautiful, at the top of the stairs.'

Thinking about it, the lady *had* been beautiful. She wouldn't mind looking like that herself if she ever got to be three hundred.

'*And* I wasn't even frightened,' she decided, shifting from her seat as a general threatening movement rippled through the class, 'until I saw what an old fashioned dress she was wearing. But then, when the silly thing turned and walked straight through the wall into Lavender, well, I just ran!'

'Lavender?' wailed a child. 'But that's my dorm!'

'And mine . . . and mine . . .' came various voices as the children gazed at one another in consternation. 'Oh! We won't *ever* be able to sleep there again.'

'Stupid girls,' came an exasperated voice from the cupboard. 'Can't you tell Kitty is making this whole thing up?' The mistress opened the door and, brushing chalk from her gown, fiddled around for her glasses. 'Now, where are my spectacles?'

'Round your neck, Miss Cowley,' offered some child hopefully, as though this at least might go some way towards solving the present crisis. 'But what are we going to *do*?'

'We are going to resume our work with as little delay as possible.'

'But the *spook*!'

There came a protracted silence. Kitty found herself thrilling to this word with a mixture of unexpected fear, excitement and disbelief all rolled into one. Had the phantom then been a *spook*? A real *spook*? Were there such things? Certainly she'd never managed to see one before, though she'd always hoped to. And now, just when she had seen one, she'd as good as gone and missed it altogether; and if no-one had actually spoken the word, she'd have carried on thinking the thing was just a rotten old phantom and not a ghost at all. For in spite of that urge to run straight to Mr Forson, who was the nearest thing to her Daddy that this place possessed, Kitty had never dared to think the thing might be truly . . . supernatural.

Now with a qualm in the tummy, Kitty felt like suddenly crying; and a tear of rage actually crept into the corner of her eye. Just to think that the thing had been a spook and she'd actually *missed* it.

'Whether or not, Kitty, you are trying to tell the truth – and you must know how I dislike fibbing – I feel it my duty to assist you to the knowledge that the existence of spooks in this school is questionable if not downright impossible.' The mistress blinked, as the girls waited with baited breath.

'Unlike the last rowdy establishment I attended, there are probably few or even *no* spooks at St Ursula's School for Girls. So I would like you all to reconsider. I really cannot stand any further disobedience in our lesson this morning. I am too old. We will return to *The Tempest*.'

'But Miss Cowley,' wailed Claudia amidst the new howl that now threatened to engulf the class entirely.

The mistress banged down her ruler savagely. '*The Tempest*, if you please!'

CHAPTER 4

From Withycombe Blaze, a pleasant village through which any visitor to the St Ursula's playing fields must first pass, a stony track climbs up into thick woods of beech, birch and pine. As it dips, climbs, dips again then finally arrives at the main road, the way may become, in a few places, little more than a muddy path; but before it does so the discerning traveller is rewarded, from a certain high ridge, by a tantalizing view of a noble Georgian façade.

In anticipation of her visit to Coxley Grange, Miss Cowley had consulted a large scale map. And despite the purpose of the mission, a nature so romantic as hers could not help experiencing a certain suppressed excitement. This did not simply relate to her future meeting with the admittedly mysterious Mr Forson. Rather, she always hoped that in her trips around the English countryside she might experience that intake of breath which in privileged circumstances occasionally accompanies the unexpected glimpse.

She therefore set off on her travels with a Byronic eagerness. The view through those shimmering new beech tresses did not fail her. With its gleam of water as yet undiscovered, this was one of those rare intimations of the miraculous.

She almost skipped down the winding woodland path to the home of Mr Forson and ultimately presented herself outside his study door. The fact that in her descent she had somehow inexplicably missed that oh! so tempting sheet of water altogether, the mistress found singularly annoying. Yet, as others before her had discovered, the American possessed an ability to disperse clouds almost before they were formed.

'Miss Cowley!' he cried, greeting her in the doorway and almost dropping his cigar in his excitement. 'At last!'

She had warned him rather sternly by telephone of her coming and had certainly not expected such warmth. Of all possible visitors, the diffident (dare we say dowdy?) Head of St Ursula's appeared at that moment the one person he really wished to see. Miss Cowley allowed her eyes to roam the extraordinary chamber with some wonder. Really, with those Remington prints of Wild West scenes, the New England colonial chairs and, above all, the silver knobbed cowhide sofa, it might all have been lifted straight from the White House itself. Abraham Lincoln glowered down at her from the wall while George Washington was busy putting his name to the Constitution.

Everything about that room shouted loudly. The decorations shouted; the fold down chairs positively screeched; while Mr Forson, leading her across to the massive drinks cabinet, was the loudest thing of all. Dressed in a Norfolk knickerbocker suit he resembled, at first glance, a member of the English gentry on a shooting party. With cheekily checked Argyll socks positively leaping from stylish two tone shoes, the result was more alarming than effective.

Yet there was something endearing about the man, something so immediately warm and honest, that she had found her defences crumbling almost before he had exclaimed, 'Oh my, but what a lovely flower you are wearing!' evidently quite as genuinely moved as she had been herself by the modest primrose.

Miss Cowley sighed. 'Do you really think so?' she murmured, and blushed faintly. 'I'm afraid I picked it on my way over here. The study of wild flowers is one of my particular hobbies.' Gazing out again at the view she added generously, 'Yes, I can indeed understand my girls finding your grounds attractive.'

Even the fact that the view now included some of those same girls prancing about on the grass could not quite destroy first impressions.

'Oh, yea. There's plenty they can do here all right: clock golf, croquet, tennis. My wife's on the court right now. Reckons the standard at St Ursula's is pretty high.'

Miss Cowley reacted. 'Is that so?'

'Yea. She's real pleased to find so many noo partners, right on tap, so to speak. Oh yes, we love it here, Miss Cowley. But that's not surprising, considering this part of the world is where we Forsons originally hailed from. I've come back to my family roots – or almost, that is.'

'Almost?'

Miss Cowley was feeling much better at the discovery of a Mrs Forson.

'Certainly. *You* know the old country seat better than I. You teach there! St Ursula's is where my family lived once upon a time. Anyway, enough of that.' He waved his hand expansively. 'Let me pour you something. Will you take your English tea, or can I offer you *quelque chose* a little stronger?' His hand was hovering around the whisky bottle (Jack Daniel's No 7, to be exact). Miss Cowley jerked back to life.

'Mr Forson,' she exclaimed. 'I regret I am not here on a social visit. I came on *quite* a different quest.'

'Oh yea? What's that?'

He handed her a sherry glass, the tawny contents of which she sipped demurely.

'It concerns the girls in my charge. Mr Forson, I feel I really have to complain . . .'

'Complain away, dear lady. But I guess you might as well sit down to do it.'

Miss Cowley sat, quite suddenly.

'Now,' she said. 'Where was I?'

Where was she indeed? She seemed all of a sudden to have forgotten her legs. She had certainly mislaid the exact details of the argument she had so carefully planned. To restore her memory, she took another sip of her sherry wine and involuntarily jerked backwards. Really, this was very strong sherry, possibly the strongest she'd ever tasted – and so dry to the palate. Presumably Americans preferred it that way. She had another swig to steady her nerves and then launched into her complaint.

Half an hour later, it was a changed person who tripped down the garden steps and out on to the front lawn. In her hand she clutched an almost empty sherry glass, and a pink glow tinged her cheek. The mistress found herself gazing with renewed ardour across the mown expanses. Though she barely touched alcohol, particularly in the afternoon, those two drinks – or was it three? – had certainly cheered her up. There was an almost girlish lilt in the usually weary voice as she enquired again:

'*What* did you say those girls are playing, Mr Forson?'

'Baseball, Miss Cowley.' Her companion spoke in a reverent tone. 'It is an American National Sport.'

'Oh – rounders!' she cried, laughing gaily. 'Well, there should not, after all, be much harm in *that*, though I fail to understand why the same thing cannot be done at school. But to return to this idea of yours about *The Tempest*. Your suggestion of using the lake begins to interest me strangely. You are convinced the play would show up well in such natural surroundings?'

'Shakespeare? Your own bard? Why, it's made for the man. Come on, I'll show you.'

Miss Cowley suddenly felt lighthearted. It was extraordinary how the American had brought up the matter of the play, and made exactly the same suggestion as that child this morning. Somehow he had contrived to discover the name of their current 'set book'. Surely, it was telepathy. With a genial nod to the blue knickered baseball players, the mistress paused only to toss back the remains of her drink before ramming the glass into her pocket and setting off across the smooth green turf in pursuit of Mr Forson.

They joined a path of mossy gravel that curved round the base of hanging woods. Fringed with those same primroses, with celandines and violets, and the first few dropping heads of the palest pink anemones, it wound enticingly between sculptured yew hedges, and Miss Cowley felt as though she were on some high cloud, drifting lightly through Paradise. The American, some way ahead, was still expostulating with boyish enthusiasm.

Miss Cowley sighed contentedly. There was Prospero's sorcery in the air, and as the lake itself appeared suddenly round the corner she fancied she heard Pan's very own pipes fluting, high above the wooded hill. What the mistress experienced next was less pleasant.

Was she mistaken, or had she made out a face – the queerest blackened sort of face – projecting malevolently over a fairly large bush, gazing down at them with such intensity that she suddenly found herself falling? From the embracing closeness of Mr Forson's strong arms she gasped:

'I distinctly heard pipes Mr Forson! And then there was a face. I saw the oddest face . . .'

'Some dryad you mean?' The American frowned. He withdrew his cigar and spat out a bit of tobacco leaf.

'No, no! It was more like . . . a *dead* thing!'

'Flip me, Miss Cowley! We mustn't allow such morbid fancies, just when we're about to make our plans.'

But the mistress was not to be fobbed off. Pushing herself away, she craned her head upward. The vision had vanished as mysteriously as it had appeared. She was quivering still as they resumed their walk and wandered to the water's edge. From here the most charming bridge had been built to span right across to the opposite bank.

'Idyllic,' she managed to stammer, the satisfying elegance of the scene serving in some slight measure to restore her nerves. 'The whole school could certainly be accommodated upon that knoll.'

She had still not agreed; but the project was tempting. Most tempting.

'Shall we? Shall we produce our *Tempest* – you and I and the girls?'

She pulled herself together and turned suddenly and impulsively to her companion. Mr Forson nodded.

'For myself, I should be more than happy, and that's a fact. My wife and I are rather lonely people, not much given to socializing. To tell the truth, Miss Cowley, those stiff and starchy County folk you have around these parts rather give me the creeps. We prefer the company of your girls. Your *girls* Miss Cowley: they are *so* natural.'

'Not mine, I fear. They are not mine. My post is only temporary.'

'Oh gee. I guess we should try to change *that*. I'll have a word with the school governors.'

'I am not sure I should wish it. I had some sudden notion this morning that I should like to retire to a fruit farm. I . . .'

'Aw! That's a pity. To be honest, I'd looked forward to a closer relationship between us.'

'Closer than what? I don't quite understand . . .'

'Miss Cowley, skip it. 'Twas no more than a passing thought. Let's get on with the play.'

She was approaching St Ursula's later, after an extended walk through the rides and ways of the closely knit woods that divide that school from the outside world, and feeling quite breathless. What was so rewarding was the way vistas kept opening up, only to be hidden again by sprays of lacy leaves that whispered, *Look at us; look at us.*

Miss Cowley was quite content to gaze at either of them. There was an exhilaration and lightness about her step that lovely evening, and she was ready to see marvels in everything around.

The Headmistress (for the first time she felt she could

legitimately use the term) had a vulnerable nature. Under that plain exterior was a heart easily moved to gratitude, and just as easily put down again. Was it the American who had made her feel so free, or simply her own inspired remarks to him? Although she knew a few compliments should not be allowed to influence a person in a position of responsibility, no-one had spoken to her so kindly for a long time. And even though she recognized how easily flattering words came to his lips, she was nevertheless daring to place all her hopes in this *Tempest* idea. It came as her first chance to contribute actively to life in St Ursula's, and Miss Cowley felt duly grateful.

She felt she owed it to Miss Devine. By taking such a positive step she would, in some measure at least, confirm the trust that her good friend had shown by granting her such high office.

The American appeared to want it. She wanted it. Most important of all, the children themselves desired to perform this wonderful play, and that, to Miss Cowley, was success! You can lead a horse to water, as the old saying goes, but you cannot make it drink. How often had the mistress tried leading her charges to the gushing fountains of knowledge? How rarely had she been able to inspire them even to take a sip? Even if the performance had really been *their* idea and not hers at all, who was Miss Cowley to complain? It was all so . . . so *natural*.

Unhappily, nature also has another side. As well as fauns and satyrs, the earth, it seems, can spew up elementals, mindless creatures of revolting aspect and spiteful mien. And that darker aspect is not easily dismissed.

Though fully aware that *all* her pleasures would sooner or later have to be paid for, Miss Cowley would have preferred to put aside indefinitely the more unpleasant incident of the face in the wood. Now, as she re-entered the school's ancient portal, the mistress received a most unwelcome reminder of a familiar who seemed to dog her footsteps; for here was Peggy Trent, a most reliable prefect, racing up to her with an expression of real horror on her face.

'Oh, Miss Cowley, thank *goodness* you're back! Tryphena Hargreaves saw the ghost just now . . .'

'What!'

'. . . or something, anyway. Oh, I *wish* you'd come and speak to her. None of the other mistresses seem to be in their rooms.'

'Where and when did you say this happened?'

'Only a moment ago – in preparation.' Peggy led the way, turning back to explain as they hurried towards the Prep Room. 'If it had been the first years again I'd have felt suspicious, but this time it's the Remove.'

The Head's heart sank. At last, it seemed, the spirits were taking their revenge. Miss Cowley did not view ghosts lightly. She had not been a member of the Redditch Poltergeist and Related Phenomena Society for nothing. It is true she had only attended their meetings for a matter of some three months. After her needlework case, her umbrella, her second best fox fur and her galoshes had all been removed one by one, seemingly by a supernatural agency, she had decided to give the Society a miss. And then when, later, she'd spotted someone with a remarkable resemblance to the 'medium' blatantly walking round the town in them, she'd almost made up her mind to go to the police. Unfortunately, during seances, the woman kept a gauze or light dishcloth over her face, so one couldn't be sure of her identity. And since Miss Cowley found it difficult to make up her mind about anything, by the time she'd reached a decision not to proceed the culprit had disappeared up the arcade and out of her life for ever. Far better to leave the spirits to those who understood their obnoxious little ways.

Imagine, therefore, her dismay this morning when that curly-haired child had recounted so glibly the story about a grey person upon the landing. Miss Cowley had tried all afternoon to put the matter out of her mind in the vague hope that it might simply have been an attempt to undermine discipline, and that the matter would die a natural death as it deserved. Now here was the frightful business cropping up all over again. Was she never to have any peace? It seemed not. Ever since her brief, but now much regretted, spell with the Society, she had felt her footsteps to be dogged by some malevolent force. That face this afternoon, it seemed, had been but a harbinger of what was to come. Miss Cowley had tampered with the unknown. Now she was being made to pay. It was with the strongest sense of foreboding that the mistress approached and entered the Remove Prep Room and glared accusingly around.

In the corner sat Tryphena, pale and shaken, with the others gathered sociably around, pointlessly fanning her with handkerchiefs and generally looking sympathetic.

'Now,' snapped Miss Cowley. 'What *is* all this?'

'Oh, Miss Cowley . . . Tryphena saw the ghost . . . a grey thing in the garden.'

'What ghost? Who's been telling you about ghosts?'

'Oh . . . haven't you heard, Miss Cowley? The school's haunted.'

'It was probably only the gardener.'

'Oh no. It wasn't Brisling. He's quite short and this person was ever so tall, didn't you say, Tryphena?'

The girl nodded dumbly, evidently paralysed with the shock. Miss Cowley pulled herself together. Really, such situations needed only the firm personality she knew she *must* possess somewhere, lurking deep down inside. Indeed, it was fortunate that she had arrived in time to deal with the matter. How would Miss Devine have behaved in similar circumstances? This was one of those situations that could get quite out of hand if it was not instantly quashed. Miss Cowley bravely proceeded to quash it now, moving unsteadily towards the black squares of window.

'You see,' she said, 'there's quite a simple answer. I just close all the curtains.'

The girls watched her closely. They seemed anything but

convinced. Peggy drew in her breath.

'Right, Jennifer. Go and get the book you want. And the rest of you, settle down.'

'It's in the dorm, Peggy. Can I take Alison and Sally with me please?'

'If you must.'

While Miss Cowley moved from window to window pulling at the curtains, the prefect watched hopelessly. And as the trio left the room, Alison too was groaning, but for rather a different reason.

'Oh, *bother* Kitty,' she muttered. '*She's* responsible for all this.'

Tryphena was one of the less imaginative members of the form, not given to making up stories. If *this* rather stolid girl had started imagining things, who knew where the matter might end?

'I really think I'd better take a look outside,' Alison sighed, 'in case there *is* a prowler.'

'Ali!' exclaimed Sally in horror, 'I don't know how you can.'

And as Alison disappeared, with that familiar worried frown, out of the door and into the topiary garden, the other two looked at one another meaningfully.

'Suppose it *is* someone,' Sally said. 'Supposing Ali gets hit on the head?'

'I wouldn't worry,' Jennifer reassured her. 'Alison knows what she's doing.'

For once, however, the leader of the Remove was mistaken. Alison had very little idea why she was wandering about out there among the shadows.

A full moon had just risen above the black bank of hillside. It resembled a mistily veiled apricot. Unlike yesterday, the air was mild, almost warm. Leaving an ivy-like trail in the dewy grass, the girl moved silently between square boxed hedges. Peering this way and that for any sign of a looming shape, she felt herself willing one into life. An owl hooted. Was she mistaken, or had she really seen something from the corner of her eye, gliding into the shadows of the kitchen garden wall?

Alison felt no fear. Instead, she experienced a curious sense of invulnerability, as though the two roles had become reversed. Now, suddenly, *she* was the hunter. The watcher had become the watched. In a second or two she was beside the wall corner, under the great yew, and feeling exactly like a wraith herself. Of course, there was nothing – only a twittering of mice in the old bricks behind. But merging into the shadow and with every nook and cranny of the garden fully visible, Alison was less interested than usual in the natural world.

Instead, she found her attention fixed on something inside the building; a still, small, bright pinpoint of light. Like a will-o-the-wisp, it was *hanging* inside the library, hovering, suspended in space. Swiftly she slid down the intervening strip of dark turf. A fairly high wall rose from a flowerbed to the level of the sill under the window that would reveal all. Had it simply been the moon's reflection, winking in the glass? No, she was sure not. Yet, when she looked, there was nothing of note. Save for a large open book on the table, all looked drearily undisturbed and very much as always in the gloom, the various volumes running in their neatly closed ranks along the shelves, just as the duty librarian for the week must have left them.

In that short space, the moon had risen an inch or two above the trees. It was now a huge gleaming silver medallion: a symbol of the never to be attained perfection. Alison sighed for the night, before slipping back indoors by way of the library passage.

Within, everything felt soggily, warmly familiar – just the sounds and smells of school. The library door was closed, yet unaccountably a strip of light showed beneath. This could be no torch. When she flung open the door, with consideration for the great black bat that might come out in a rush of flapping wings, all the lights were full on, blazing away with apparently no-one to see, and it was the nastiest sensation to be there at all. Yet she could not stop herself entering.

Beneath a glaring bulb lay the open tome. She glanced at the cover: *The Legends and History of Semley Hall.* There was a slight sound. Someone was creeping up behind her . . .

'Hello, Alison dear,' said a voice quietly enough, and Alison nearly leapt out of her skin.

'Oh Verity! You gave me such a shock.'

'Why? What's up?' Verity crossed over from her shelf, face creased with interest and suspicion. Really, there was no need to cover the book, but as though it were her own private property, Alison found herself doing so. Verity wrested the volume from her.

'What's this?'

It was a book. Anyone could see that. What a pain you are Verity Lamton, Alison thought irritably.

'Were you in here with a torch just now?

'With a torch? Whatever for?'

It was just at that second that they heard a scream. For a moment, both girls looked at each other as if paralysed. Then they ran.

Jennifer was lying in a tumbled heap on the floor at the bottom of their dormitory steps, with several girls bending over her inert body, gazing in horror and disbelief. Sally looked up, her face ashen.

'Oh glory,' she whispered. 'She's dead.'

Alison dropped to her knees and listened to the erratic heartbeat.

'No she's not. She's just fainted. Get Miss Devine – I mean Matron.'

A surging collection of girls ran off, while Sally, Alison and Verity remained.

'What's happened, Sally?' said Verity.

'I can't tell you.'

'Leave her alone,' said Alison.

'I will not leave her alone. Can't you see she's upset?'

The words took Alison's breath away.

'So why don't you leave her alone?'

'That's right,' Sally sobbed, 'carry on talking between

yourselves. Go on talking as if I wasn't here. I'm just a bit of wood after all . . .'

'Well, what d'you mean, you *can't* tell us? *Why* can't you tell us?' Verity persisted. 'Was it your fault?'

'No, it wasn't my fault.'

'Then why all the mystery, eh? What are you covering up?'

'For the last time, Verity,' shouted Alison, 'what on earth's it got to do with you?'

'Good gracious, Alison Dayne! You've only been at this school eighteen months and already you talk as if you own the place . . .'

Fortunately, at this point, the conversation was interrupted. The matron and Miss Terson, the duty mistress for the night, had arrived and, together with many helping hands, they carried the inert body of Jennifer upstairs.

During the procedure, Verity fell in with Rachel Adams. They disappeared together, in deep conversation, just before the party reached the San. Jen was deposited in bed. Miss Terson turned to Peggy.

'Try to calm everyone down, there's a love. We'll cancel the rest of Prep,' she called after the retreating figure.

Sally looked up tearfully.

'Will she be all right?'

'Who? Peggy?'

'No. Jennifer, I mean.'

'Too early to say. Any bones broken, Nurse?'

'We won't have done her much good humping her about, if there are,' remarked the matron cheerfully.

This brought a fresh wave of tears.

'Oh dear. Oh dear. Whatever have I done?'

'What *have* you done?' asked Miss Terson.

'Nothing!' Alison had her arm round her friend's heaving shoulders.

'Then why are you bawling?' enquired the mistress in exasperation. 'Look.' She drew the girl to one side. 'I'd like to talk to you alone, but it isn't my place. We'll have to go to Miss

Cowley.' The duty mistress winced slightly. 'And you, Alison. You'd better come along.'

Trembling in every limb, Sally followed Miss Terson into Miss Devine's study. Alison hurried after them.

Miss Cowley sat there at her desk, staring fixedly at the telephone.

'Now,' said Miss Terson. 'What happened?'

Sally covered her face with her hands. 'Oh,' she shuddered, looking at Alison through slightly parted fingers. 'It was just *too* horrible.'

The deputy Head rose. She walked unsteadily round the desk then, tentatively planting a hand on the head of fair hair, murmured, for want of anything better, 'These things will happen, my dear.'

Miss Terson sighed. 'Come on. What was too horrible? Jennifer falling?'

'No. The thing in the dorm.'

Both mistresses visibly stiffened.

'The thing in the dorm? Whatever do you mean?'

Sally gulped. 'We were nipping up there for a book. Jennifer had asked Alison and me to go with her because Tryphena had seen something queer in the garden.'

'Go on.'

Trying to detect any evidence of falsehood, the duty mistress looked closely at the girl. Sally's distress was obvious, but was she merely trying to cover up some shameful misconduct? Running, for instance, or pushing, shoving, tripping? Would they never learn about those treacherously polished floors? Gulping, the girl began to dry her eyes.

'Well,' she said, calmer at last. 'We'd gone into the dormitory. Jennifer wasn't sure where to look, and I was pretty jumpy after all that stuff downstairs, so we pressed the light switch.'

'Yes?' said Miss Cowley faintly.

'I pressed down the switch, but the wretched thing didn't come on at all.' There was a pregnant pause. Miss Cowley was trying to do something with her ear – get wax out possibly. They all watched as she probed inside.

'I said: "Blow. The bulb's gone",' the girl continued. 'Jennifer said she thought she'd left the book on her bed. I say, are you all right Miss Cowley?'

'Yes, I'm all right,' replied the husky voice. 'I think I might just sit down again, however.'

They watched the deputy headmistress grope her way round the desk as though here, too, the light had failed, and then fall into her chair.

'There was no illumination whatever, you say, and yet . . . you still saw . . . something?'

'Yes. Our eyes were getting used to the darkness by then. I was going to walk away, because there was the queerest atmosphere in that dorm, but Jennifer uttered a piercing scream . . .'

'Why?'

'Why what?'

'Why did she scream? Are you sure you hadn't been working yourselves up into a state because of the supposed thing in the garden?'

Miss Terson knew the girls and their hysterical tendencies. Once started, a mood could spread like a forest fire.

'Of course not,' Sally snapped crossly. 'We both saw it. We wouldn't both imagine the same thing at exactly the same moment, would we?'

'It has been known,' exlaimed Miss Cowley, suddenly and unexpectedly coming back to life. 'I refer of course to the collective hallucination . . . a phenomenon well enough reported by trustworthy observers to establish its undoubted authenticity . . .'

'But *what* did you see?' Miss Terson interrupted in exasperation.

'Didn't I tell you?'

'No, you did not.'

'You mean I haven't even mentioned yet about that

horrible, horrible grey thing looming at us from the corner like a . . . like . . .' Sally furiously scratched her head.

'Like a what?'

'Well . . . like a monk . . . like an immensely tall hooded *monk*, but with its back to us. We didn't wait around to see any more, I can tell you. We just ran back screaming down the passage.' There was a pause. 'I suppose,' she finished lamely, 'we should have walked.'

It was Miss Terson's turn to sink into a chair.

'What are we going to do?'

'You won't make us sleep there?'

'Of course we won't make you sleep there, poor child,' said Miss Cowley, turning with reproach to her colleague.

'*I* never said they had to,' retorted the duty mistress.

'Oh crumbs,' Alison muttered.

'Though I should like to know where they *are* to sleep,' added Miss Terson, tersely enough.

'In the sanatorium?' Miss Cowley murmured.

'All of them? They can't *all* go. There isn't room.'

'Yes, they must *all* go to the sanatorium,' decided Miss Cowley with unusual firmness, 'if necessary lying on palliases. There can be no question of anyone being subjected to a recurrence of such a horror.'

'What are we to tell them? What reasons are we to give?'

'That the dormitory is being decorated.'

'In the middle of the night?'

'Certainly. It will be like the railways closing down for works, when everyone most wishes to use them. On Sunday.'

'I don't mind staying in the dorm,' interrupted Alison quietly. 'Sally can go in with Jennifer and then no-one'll suspect anything.'

'Good Heavens, child, what a suggestion!' Miss Cowley inflated, her breast quivering with indignation. 'Suppose there is an escaped lunatic up there?' It was possible. Anything was possible.

'You could get Mr Brisling to look first,' Miss Terson snapped.

'Mr Brisling! From what I have seen of him, I hardly think it fair to subject one so stricken in years to er . . . to er . . .'

'Ring Farquhar.'

'What?'

'I said ring Farquhar.'

'*Major* Farquhar?' enquired Miss Cowley coldly.

'There is no other, Miss Cowley. He's the one who decides things while Miss Devine's away.'

'What!' Miss Cowley's jaw had sagged open. The duty mistress had spoken unequivocally, off-handedly almost, using the same words as that child had done this morning. Evidently they all thought she was quite useless and absolutely unnecessary in the school, a mere figurehead: no more, no less.

'I shall not ring Major Farquhar,' she replied feebly.

'Then I shall.' The duty mistress seized the instrument. 'It's about time that interfering old idiot was put on the spot.'

Slightly mollified, Miss Cowley listened. It was a lengthy conversation. Try as she might, she could not *hear* what the frightful man was saying about her; but it was not necessary to use too much imagination. Yes, he *had* been eating his dinner, and yes, this *would* all happen while Miss Devine was away. Never an admirer of Miss Devine (the Major had been the lone dissenting voice at her election five years ago), he was even less one of Miss Cowley. What the school needed was discipline. *This* was exactly the kind of thing the school didn't need. A few more ghosts and they'd have a riot on their hands. No, he hadn't the slightest idea what to do, except give 'em all a good beating and send 'em to bed on bread and water, the lot of 'em. The phone went down.

'He's flummoxed.' Miss Terson spoke with satisfaction. 'He's going to ring back . . .'

'Oh dear. Was he bad tempered?' Miss Cowley asked anxiously.

'Quite bad tempered, yes.'

'Will he send for the police?'

'Quite possibly.'

'Excuse me butting in,' said Sally, 'but I think I'll pop up and see if Jennifer's come out of her fainting fit now, if that's all right?'

'Go ahead, dear,' replied Miss Terson vaguely. 'You can make your sleeping arrangements with Matron at the same time.'

'Are you coming, Ali?'

'No. I think I'll stay in the dorm tonight.'

'Well, it's your choice, of course,' Sally snapped.

'I'm afraid I think there *is* no choice,' explained Alison with care, and the others all turned to listen. 'Obviously the suggestion about the dormy being decorated wouldn't be taken seriously' (Miss Cowley cleared her throat at this point) 'and there's no other reason for leaving that I can think of, that isn't going to start everyone panicking again.' She turned to her friend. 'I'm frightfully sorry, Sally, about Jennifer, and I don't want to pour cold water on your story . . .'

'I should hope not!' retorted that person stiffly, her hand on the door.

'Is something wrong, dear?' Miss Cowley enquired.

Sally shook her head. No. Nothing was wrong, except she, Sally Spencer, was once again being made to look a fool and a deserter. She wasn't going to sleep in that rooom, however, not if they paid her. Alison continued inexorably:

'No-one's ever seen anything up there before now. Ghosts don't usually appear twice in the same night – do they?'

Miss Terson shrugged.

'Well, they don't, actually.' Alison was trying to muster some common sense at last in this ludicrous situation, and she preferred not to have her train of thought broken. It was quite mad. Here were two grown women willing to listen to anything that might solve this potty problem. Alison felt in the midst of one of her queerer sorts of dreams.

'Go, if you're going,' Miss Terson told Sally irritably.

Evidently troubled, Sally went.

'All the *real* ghosts I've ever heard of,' Alison continued doggedly, 'only come once or twice to the same person. I mean, after they've been seen, they don't appear again for ages. Perhaps you *should* send up Mr Brisling to see if there's an escaped lunatic, but when you find there isn't . . . well, I don't think it's worth upsetting the rest of the girls any more. Nobody'll think Sally's odd wanting to be with Jen.'

'Sounds like common sense to me,' Miss Terson admitted. 'Shall I inform the Major?'

She was just about to place her hand on the phone when the thing rang, and Miss Terson sprang back before reapproaching and cautiously lifting the receiver. It was a wise move, as it happened. The voice at the other end was loud enough to be heard in the yard.

'It's Mr Forson!' gasped Miss Cowley in exitement. 'Give me that phone! Mr Forson?'

'Good to hear you, Miss Cowley. Say, I've just been told about your little problem over there. I can't tell you how sorry I am.'

'Mr Forson . . . I can explain.'

'No need, dear lady. I'd already heard your school was haunted, from some kid yesterday: it's some old dame in grey, apparently. Now I guess it's only a rumour, or that some brat is playing a stoopid joke, but until it all blows over I want you to send your girls here right away to Coxleys. We've got so much dormitory space upstairs in this place, we don't know what to do with it.'

'Tomorrow,' Miss Terson hissed. 'Say tomorrow.'

'Well, that's very good of you. How about tomorrow?'

'If you insist . . . tomorrow then. It'll give them time to collect their things, but at this moment – well, please try to calm yourself, Miss Cowley.'

'I am perfectly calm now.'

'I know you are. I can hear that. Have you told 'em about the play yet?'

'First thing in the morning I intend to begin devising a notice.'

'Good! Let *me* tell *you* something nice. I'm building a raft for the first scene. Isn't that exciting? It'll give them *all* something real nice to think about. I guess that's what they need right now. My goodness, Miss Cowley, I don't know what that school would do without a Headmistress of your calibre to look after it. It's OK having a whole lotta broads all together at one gulp, but in the great drama of life I guess we need strong hands at the tiller, and in you, Miss Cowley, we've got them. I was just telling the Major . . . yes Maam!'

Mr Forson had evidently replaced his receiver, for the voice ceased as quickly as it had begun.

'Well,' Miss Cowley exulted, staring at the instrument with unalloyed satisfaction, 'did you just hear what that dear man said?'

CHAPTER 5

It was the following afternoon.

Mr Brisling had duly made his inspection the previous night, grumbling as he went and telling various mistresses to stand back and get out of the way. He had then kicked open the door and trundled inside like a wheezing battering ram. Not unexpectedly, all had been calm in Primrose Dorm.

A little later, Verity Lamton had been busy discussing with Tryphena Hargreaves a forthcoming visit to the theatre in London.

'I've always rather fancied offering them my services, to tell you the truth,' she had volunteered magnanimously. 'I reckon I'd do it rather well, don't you?'

In fact she'd been so busy visualizing herself in a leading West End role that she'd barely had time to enquire further about Jennifer's accident. She was saving that up.

Now it was already four o'clock next day and everyone except Alison had slept like tops – for most of the afternoon, certainly. Greek, Latin and French all together – what an indigestible mixture! Alison, half dead with fatigue, felt fractious. Verity, on the other hand, had spent the morning at the dentist and the afternoon at her music lesson in Stalminster.

Bees hummed laconically around the old school porch, while inside all was activity. *All* the Remove, it seemed, was bound that afternoon for Coxley Grange, not simply the members of Primrose Dorm. But while others set off into the sunshine armed with tennis rackets, Alison and Sally, like refugees, were lumping suitcases across the hall.

Verity was waiting for them, surrounded by a noisy crowd of Juniors. They found her even more encumbered than themselves, since the girl had to take her violin with her everywhere. She hailed them.

'Rather exciting, what, all this . . . I *don't* think.'

'What's all the row?' Sally growled. 'Has the place gone stark raving mad?'

'Haven't you seen the notice board?' Kitty beamed as they fought their way through the scrum.

Sally edged herself to the front of the crowd and read: 'Apart from those temporarily quartered there, and anyone involved in rehearsals for the proposed outdoor production of *The Tempest* by William Shakespeare, only girls wishing to play tennis or rounders are to be allowed into the grounds of Coxley Grange!'

The notice was signed: 'Margaret Cowley, Acting Headmistress.'

'Well!' gasped Sally. 'As notices go, that one certainly takes the biscuit.'

'It means we can still play about over there, all of us, just the same as before, doesn't it?' Claudia Hiram asked, jumping up and down. Why could these children never keep still for a minute?

'Quite evidently . . .' came Verity's sardonic voice from the background. 'So what the thump was the point in writing anything?'

'*What* mooted production of *The Tempest*?' Sally enquired as they set off for the great outdoors, with their belongings.

'Something Mr Forson suggested,' Alison muttered.

'I'm in it,' Kitty shouted after the departing trio. 'I'm going to be Ariel. Come on, Claudia. I'll show you what I thought I might wear over my liberty bodice.'

'I suppose it's Miss Cowley's way of taking their minds off spooks,' observed Verity. 'Pretty feeble, I must say. How *is* Jennifer, by the bye?'

'If you must know,' Sally replied coldly, 'there's pretty bad concussion.' If her tone of voice was meant to discourage further probing on the subject, however, it had little effect. Verity was made like a golf ball: petite and wonderfully elastic.

'Oh dear,' she murmured sympathetically, 'that can so often mask the most ghastly things.'

'Thanks, Verity, for those few kind words.'

'I'm only trying to be realistic.'

'Rot.'

'Well, if you ask me . . .'

'We don't,' came the concerted reply. Alison and Sally had met Miss Terson during the afternoon. Both had agreed to keep quiet about the 'monk', to cast him back into the dark corner where he belonged.

'If you ask me,' Verity began again evenly with the patient tone a governess might use when dealing with two naughty children, 'I agree with the "Person". It wouldn't have been allowed in *Prosey*'s day.' (Prosey being of course 'Prosey Prosser' the extremely unpopular second mistress, enemy of Alison Dayne, who had left the school over a year ago under such a cloud.)

'For Pete's sake, Verity,' Alison cried, goaded beyond endurance, 'what's the matter with you? Anyone can trip on some stairs.'

'For no reason?' Verity smiled in her most superior manner and turned in at the gates of Coxley's. 'Mind you don't trip yourself, Alison, my precious; that's all I can say to *you*.'

Alison barely listened to the taunt. As she wandered on past the still glaring gardener towards the big house, she was reminded again of the child who had unwittingly begun all this palaver.

'Oh, I do feel a complete traitor coming over here like this,' she murmured to herself.

Deserting the school! Alison felt suddenly (and quite unreasonably) as though St Ursula's were beginning to disintegrate physically. Indeed, some cracks in the building *had* already appeared, under the ivy along the back wall. It probably didn't mean anything. But she'd noticed them the other day.

Deserting the school! Taking advantage of Miss Devine's absence, it was as if the Fates had decided St Ursula's should come to an end. And since Kitty had been their first unknowing tool, it was somehow up to Alison to put matters right. Then, as if echoing her thoughts, Verity, walking ahead, shouted back:

'I know one thing. If I'd been Miss Devine, *I* wouldn't have left the old place to go waltzing off to Bosnavia just when I was needed. I'd have stayed behind where my duty lay.'

'She wasn't needed *then*,' Alison snorted, catching the other two up. 'And attending her brother's Coronation can hardly be called "waltzing off".' As they came into the shadows of the Grange itself, Sally's face brightened.

'Actually,' she exclaimed, her face alight, 'why don't we *demand* to stay in the old dorm?'

It was as if a weight had been lifted from her mind. While Alison had stuck it out there, last night, she, on the other hand, had deserted 'Primrose' in its hour of crisis.

'Stay there!' Verity plonked down her cases. 'After what *you* saw?'

Taken completely by surprise, Sally stiffened. Then she expanded like a startled frog. 'Why, you precious duffer! What *did* we see?'

Aloofly, Verity picked up her cases again and walked round the house towards the front entrance.

'My dear pet idiot, there was obviously some absurd reason for us all to be moved over here so suddenly in such a panic.'

'You heard the reason, you ass. They're going to decorate the ceiling.'

'Straight away - today - just like that, without any prior warning?' Verity snorted derisively. 'What d'you take me for? The paint's brand new. Still, I must admit Jennifer's done us quite a favour. Simply look at the place.'

It was true that, when regarded from this point, Coxley Grange certainly had its attractions. Rooks cawed noisily in the ancient elms, ducks quacked happily on the lake, while the building itself seemed to be preening its feathers that warm afternoon. Built to face south, its mellow stone front reflected the sun through trailing clematis and exotically blooming camellias.

While the plop of the ball wafted from the tennis court, the click of a harder and smaller ball emanated from under a spreading chesnut. Clock golf was in progress on the freshly hoovered lawn. Hearing the sound of apparent disharmony over there on the gravel, Mr Forson straightened with a frown.

He did not wish to hear argument. Such dissonance grated on this fine, sunny afternoon, for the American had taken some pride in the new luxurious dormitory space. The beds were more inviting, more daintily covered than a Bosnavian Princess's, while the carpet was thick enough to shear. He had personally supervised the flower arrangements, having had blooms sent over from the hothouse that very morning. Under the eaves sparrows twittered noisily over nesting sites. These girls, too, were supposed to be nesting. They were supposed to be thrilled by the prospect of settling into Coxley's, not bawling their heads off before they'd even seen what he'd done for them.

'Back in a mo, sweeties.' Mr Forson left his game with a frown and a snap of the tongue.

'Golly, Verity Lamton,' Sally was shouting, 'That's treachery – don't you realize? You're an unfaithful, beastly turncoat.'

'Spongebags!'

'Hi, girls! Everything sweetness and light?'

The voice of the millionaire sounded casual as always. But with Verity Lamton glaring at him, the absence of sweetness and light was both obvious and decidedly unnerving.

In fact the air was so frosty that even this warm hearted benefactor felt himself wilting like one of his own orchids. Under that thick skin, Mr Forson possessed an unexpectedly sensitive nature. Getting no reaction whatever from the girls, he just about managed to shrug, then said:

'Oh well, I've tried to make your new dormitory hunky dory. Here's hoping anyway . . .' And to prove that he wasn't hurt, Mr Forson bit firmly on his cigar then simulated a fair exhibition of jauntiness on his way up the steps. He had not meant to go into the house at all. The three looked blankly after him for a moment, then Sally turned.

'Verity, love, don't sneak,' she pleaded. 'We've promised, Guide's honour, to play all this horrid ghost business down. Surely you must understand?'

'Pish,' hissed the irascible Verity. 'You're simply trying to protect your own precious skins - yours and that Kitty's, too.'

Her olive branch thrust back in her teeth, Sally's mouth compressed to a hard line. The tears were again not far away.

'Well, my sainted giddy aunt! I like that! It's *you* we're thinking about, you utter ass - you and everyone else at St Ursula's. Oh, I wish I'd never sent Jen away.'

'Eh?' blinked Alison.

'When Teddy came to tea. Everything's been so horrible since. I don't think I can bear another minute of it!'

Flinging down her bags, the girl flew across the gravel and away after Mr Forson up the steps.

Verity turned to Alison with a pained expression.

'*Now* look what you've done,' she declared, and Alison's jaw dropped.

Why were they all at each other's throats? Were Miss Cowley's forebodings true? Was the escaped lunatic one of *them*? Or was the school under some sort of curse?

Perversely enough, by contrast, Miss Cowley had been quite cheery all afternoon. Most of the day, indeed, she had been planning her forthcoming Shakesperian production, pacing about her study and occasionally throwing her hands in the air and laughing.

As Headmistress, Miss Cowley was not expected to teach. The sixth she took for French; and, along with all the other mistresses, managed her stint with these frightful first years. Now, this following morning, she faced them almost jauntily. A piece of ink-soaked blotting paper, which she deftly avoided, flew past her ear and splattered harmlessly against the blackboard.

'Quiet,' she cried, in a genial voice. 'Quiet, children please. This is not the House of Commons or a zoo.'

The form subsided fractionally. They wanted good news. Miss Cowley, they felt sure, could be relied on to supply that news. There were important matters to discuss. One of these was ghosts. For now that it was generally accepted that the school was haunted, even the smallest girls, who might otherwise have remained fairly vague on the subject, were anxious to catch up on the most newsworthy news the school had ever had.

It was not usual to find their mistresses ruffled in the way they'd been these last few days. The discomfiture was deeply interesting to observe. If Alison hated the idea of the break-up of St Ursula's, the first years had no such qualms. They positively revelled in it.

So unless Miss Cowley could come up with some alternative and more powerful attraction this particular Tuesday morning, the possibility of keeping the imps under control looked doubtful. The mistress, however, faced the lesson with confidence. She felt she had that alternative within her grasp. Miss Cowley had *The Tempest* with which to tempt and, aflame herself with eagerness for the project, she wished similarly to fire the imagination of these girls. If she wanted them to share in that positively creative experience, it was not simply to rid them of the unhealthy ghost obsession that at the moment seemed to have such a grip on their destructive young minds. (There could be, Miss Cowley had finally decided, only one reason for the appearance of *that* ghastly and awesome monkish figure: it was that ghosts breed ghosts in the minds of the illiterate. The Devil finds work for idle minds as well as for the idle hands that were now engaged in flicking bits of paper.) With determination she rapped on the table.

'You will all be pleased to hear that Mr Forson has suggested we perform *The Tempest* on his charming lake at Coxley's, and that I have accepted his invitation.'

She waited anxiously for the response. They had been expecting her to explain about ghosts. She was not explaining anything. For a moment, their reaction hung suspended in the dusty air. Then it came – thankfully, a roar of absolute approval.

'Hurrah!' they shouted. 'Well done, MooCow! Just what we wanted! Good old Miss Cowley! Oh, I can't wait to audition for Prospero – I'll play Miranda – No! *I'm* Miranda. You can be Gonzalo – That old buzzard? You must be joking, fishface – You look more like Caliban, if you want to know the truth about yourself – Ya! Gammon! I'd rather know the truth about you 'cos . . .'

'Girls, please! I am *trying* to speak. This will give us . . . GIRLS. This will give us,' she croaked, this time almost catching the frog in her throat and casting him from her for ever – 'the most wonderful opportunity to translate the lifeless printed page into real drama. Do not take that too literally, Nesta, *please.*'

The girl who had sprung into the air, throwing her head back like a jack-in-the-box, sat down and asked meekly, 'Is there a ghost in it, Miss Cowley?'

'Good Heavens!' the mistress gargled as she struggled to keep above water. 'Hasn't there already been enough talk of ghosts?'

'Sorry, Miss Cowley. I just thought that if there *were* one in the play, our ghost could act the part . . .'

The form tittered. Miss Cowley, even now prepared to compromise, allowed:

'There are certain spirits, of course . . . fauns, satyrs; elves of marshland and ferny brake; of standing water and wooded hill.' A slow smile crossed her face in spite of herself.

'You mean sprites,' Kitty explained to her, 'like Ariel. He's a kind of ghost. Oh, I do so want to play that part, Miss Cowley. I've got the right sort of face for it. My cousin said so.'

'Pooh,' Claudia glared. 'I've just told you, you look more like a monster . . .'

'Claudia – you're a horrible creature.'

'No, listen,' shouted Mabel Goodyear. 'Mr Parkinson ought to be Caliban.'

'I want to be Trinculo,' Nesta declared, springing on to her seat and speaking in a deep voice.

Miss Cowley cleared her throat nervously.

'Girls. Girls. I am afraid I have made a decision that is bound to be unpopular. As I want this to be the school's best production ever, the main parts must go to older girls than yourselves.'

'But that's . . . *treachery,*' cried Nesta after a long pause. 'You can't *do* it Miss Cowley.'

'I'm afraid I can.'

'We won't learn anything if those beastly stuck up seniors

get all the best parts,' wailed Laura Fanning. 'It's our beastly set book. It should be *our* play!'

The agreement was unanimous. The fury of the crowd was now unleashed on the poor unwitting victim in the stocks. Together with words like feeble, stingy and rotter, pencils, pellets, rubbers flew across the room – anything the mob could lay their hands on.

The mistress clapped her hands over her ears. The image of her sister's fruit farm flickered before her eyes. Yes; she had it – fixed in her mind as clearly and soothingly as ever. Into that peaceful scene four little lambs had just gambolled – two black and two white – past the old English sheepdog she had put there last time, and the geese from the time before. *Her* sheep would never be sent to the butcher, of course. They were there for their pure new wool, and the garments Miss Cowley would knit from it during the twilit months of winter – black pullovers from the black sheep, white ones from the white.

While the clamour raged within, however, footsteps might have been heard outside in the corridor, tramping steadily and in unison towards the classroom. The door was suddenly snatched open. Into the bedlam walked two people. One was a military looking gentleman. The other resembled, for want of a better description, a person of the female type.

'Oooh!' someone gasped.

Kitty paused from hitting Claudia over the head with her earless rabbit. Those standing on desks slid quietly back into their seats. From the form generally came a dying hiss, as of a tyre going down. It was the prelude to absolute silence.

'Yes, oooh!' echoed a sarcastic female voice. 'What are these toys on the desks? Away with them. I've never known such behaviour. Now. Where is your Headmistress?'

Philippa put up her hand.

'If you please, Bosnavia . . .'

'Foolish child. I am not referring to Miss Devine. I mean your deputy Head, Miss Cowley. We were told we would find her here.'

The members of the first form glanced nervously at each other. Claudia ventured:

'She's in the map cupboard at the moment I b'lieve . . .'

'Come now, do not be impertinent,' the female voice retorted. 'What would a mistress be doing in a cupboard?'

Never one to see storms ahead, Kitty piped up:

'Perhaps she's frightened of the ghost?'

There was just the faintest snigger. It was a snigger ill advised. The form shrank back in their seats at the answering expression on the female person's face. Boding ill, a pair of gimlet eyes bored into that hapless child and, in a brave attempt to put matters right, Theresa Fenstake added hastily:

'It's a kind of punishment, I think.'

'A punishment?' came the astonished reply. 'To lock *herself* in a cupboard?' The visitor gazed in disbelief at her companion who, having just slightly inclined his head, pursed a pair of military lips and clasped his neatly gloved hands.

'I suppose she's trying to show us up for what little beasts we really are,' explained Mabel Goodyear. 'At least, that's what she was saying when I last saw her.'

The military man seemed faintly amused by this. Not so the female person. After the cold bleak eyes had raised themselves for a long moment to the ceiling, their owner crossed briskly to the cupboard. She rapped twice.

'Is there anyone inside?'

Reply came there none. The question was rephrased.

'If there *is* anyone within, pray, may the door be opened?'

The cupboard door edged outwards just a fraction. Then, quite sharply, it opened.

'Yes?' said its inhabitant.

The deputy Head stood composed and erect within.

'Miss Cowley, I presume?' responded the newcomer's acid-drop voice.

'That is correct.' Leaving the farm behind for another day, another crisis, the mistress stepped forth with dignity and calm and gravely inclined her head.

'I would like to introduce you to Major Farquhar, Chairman of our Governors.'

'We have met,' Miss Cowley replied drily.

'My own name is Prosser. I have returned to this school to fill the vacant post of second mistress.'

An audible sigh escaped the class at the feared and hated name of this person whom they had heard about on many occasions but were meeting for the first time ever. The response that rose to Miss Cowley's lips sounded more like a howl of pain.

'*What?*' she screeched. In a wild attempt to recover some last few shreds of self respect, she managed to stammer, 'Why was I not informed?'

'Yes, yes. A good question.' The Major polished his eye glass and then replaced it. 'But do not allow yourself to think for a moment that we did not give the matter our fullest consideration. Why, you will be asking yourself, were you not invited to the meeting of the Board? Quite so. Why indeed? Ah . . .' The Major's plain flat face broke into a plain flat smile as he thought about the answer. 'Teaching and so forth . . . we simply thought we wouldn't put you to any more trouble after that most unfortunate affair. The girl Jennifer Soames will not, I regret to say, be returning to the school for the time being. I understand her mother and father are in quite a state.'

'And,' the Prosser woman added in menacing tone, 'from what I've seen of discipline here, it won't be long before other parents write to complain. Some girls appear frightened out of their wits.'

'We decided to bring back Miss Prosser, don't you know. Since she has a reputation for dealing with this kind of thing . . . thought it rather a good notion. Well . . .' Major Farquhar cleared his throat, 'won't waste any more of your valuable time, Miss Cowley. Good morning.'

After passing a hand over a dampened brow, the harassed Major strode out of the door. Goodness, he was glad *that* was over. Most embarrassing. Miss Prosser, however, remained. For a moment she allowed her gaze to play once more over the tautened faces of the form. It was enough to chill each heart. Vampires were as nothing compared to Miss Prosser.

'I shall be listening to you,' she murmured in the quietest, most threatening voice they had ever heard. And there came not a single disruptive peep from the first form at St Ursula's for the rest of that unhappy morning.

Over a year had passed since Miss Prosser's ignominious flight from St Ursula's School for Girls. You may remember the story of her involvement in the alarming episode of the fire, and Alison Dayne's heroism in saving Stephen Devine.

Be assured that Miss Prosser also remembered, with a mixture of shame and otherwise unmitigated anger. For in spite of everything that had happened, the ex-second mistress remained convinced of Alison's essential guilt. It was Miss Prosser's firm belief that the girl came of bad stock and that, as a punishment for gross insubordination, she should have been expelled. Miss Prosser's conviction was as sure now as at the moment when she had turned the key on the blazing sanatorium block.

How she had cursed herself for having panicked and run away. She had not wanted her enemy to die in the flames – perish the thought. Behind that leathery exterior lay a misunderstood pride that had taken a lot of beatings over the years, and it was that pride which had been her downfall.

For, in her heart, Miss Prosser knew she had not had the courage to own up and confess, as she would have expected any girl to do if faced with similar circumstances. How much trouble might have been saved, had she done just that. She would have been spared the humiliation of having to return to her old and much despised job as a governess, for a start. The last pair of brats had been abominations.

How welcome then had been the Major's telephone message.

Up till a week ago no-one had had any idea of her whereabouts, not the slightest hint. Then, when she had read in the local newspaper about Miss Devine's Bosnavian nonsense, Miss Prosser decided the moment she had been waiting for had at last arrived.

She had written a short, discreet letter to her old ally on the Board offering her services . . . 'should they be needed in this time of uncertainty'. She was assuming the times were uncertain. It was a gamble. Miss Prosser herself remained the uncertain one. But the throw was lucky so far. The Major welcomed that note as a direct intervention by the Gods.

Miss Prosser's future appeared suddenly in a very different light indeed. If she could just manage to re-establish herself as indispensable before Miss Devine's return, how would the Headmistress ever be able seriously to contemplate throwing her out again? The appointment was to be temporary. That was the agreement. Miss Prosser had other, darker plans. If the Head failed to comply with her request for a permanent post in her old role as second mistress . . . then, who knew?

Oh, how satisfying it was to feel that in their moment of crisis it was to *her* the Govenors had turned. They had evidently realized at long last that only Miss Prosser could quell this present unholy riot. She would behave with the utmost care and discretion, but what an amazing vindication of her stand to know the present crisis had been caused by Alison Dayne's cousin, thus proving her theories about the whole family. The mistress trembled. She rubbed her hands with glee. But she had to suppress that self-righteous indignation, for this time, she knew, she dared not put a foot wrong.

Having had the whole situation explained, Miss Prosser knew instantly what her first move must be. It must be to stop the rot where it had begun – with this interfering American fellow. The Cowley woman was of little importance. It could not be long before Miss Devine returned to St Ursula's. The whole school must be gathered together immediately. She would have to act fast . . .

It was later that day. An extraordinary general assembly had been called. At this very moment, indeed, girls were already amassed in the hall. Yet where *was* Alison Dayne? Sally had hunted everywhere. When she finally burst into the library, it was to find her friend, of all things, immersed again in that silly old book. Stinging jellyfish! Had the idiot not heard the news? She couldn't have done. Sally herself had only spotted the terrible black shape a moment ago in the corridor.

'Come *on*,' she screeched. 'They're all in there already. We'll be late. You'll never guess why – something incredible!'

'Why then?'

Alison kept her finger on her place as she looked up. She would go to assembly, but nothing could be so incredible as what she had just read in that book.

'Prosey's back.'

'*What*!'

She leapt to her feet, all the colour drained from her cheeks. But then they changed to a flaming red. 'You're making a joke!'

'I'm not, I swear. Come and see for yourself.'

'It's incredible,' Alison was still muttering bitterly as, heads bowed, Sally and she stood together in the back row. 'Absolutely beyond belief . . .'

The other girl had had little to do with the Triumphant Three during that first term of Alison's school career. She had not even been in the same form. This was no reason to deny her heartfelt agreement to that dour observation. Miss Prosser's role during the period was known to everyone and their condemnation of that role unanimous. But there was no time for further discussion.

Before them on the dais sat a cowed Miss Cowley, an equally defeated Head Girl and a glitteringly triumphant Prosser. Prosser rose.

'Stand up, Kitty Dayne,' rang out her voice instantly. Amidst dismay and sympathy, the child did as she was bid. To Kitty, an entirely new dimension was at that moment added to a hitherto blithe and unfaltering existence.

'Very well,' proceeded the silky smooth voice of the new mistress, 'I shall not mince words. I do not have time. I will simply say – the position of second mistress being concerned primarily with discipline – that I feel it my duty to eradicate immediately the present rumour at St Ursula's about *ghosts*. There are no such things as ghosts. There never were, and there never will be – not while *I* am here, at any rate. Kitty! Is that *quite* clear?'

'Yes, Miss Prosser.'

'In that case, you may sit. In a moment the whole school will form an orderly crocodile and file along behind myself to search out every nook and cranny of this building. And if anyone finds a ghost, I am willing to give that person five hundred lines and a detention every Saturday for the rest of term. Is that understood?'

No-one answered. This meeting had been called at a moment's notice. They were all still too much in a state of shock to reply to Miss Prosser's rhetorical questions.

'Now, to minor matters. I have been asked by Miss Cowley to confirm that the rehearsals of *The Tempest* are postponed indefinitely. This is because of our joint decision to make, from now on, the grounds of Coxley Grange *out of bounds*.'

No-one except Miss Cowley moved a muscle. Miss Cowley, however, sat bolt upright. There had been no joint decision on anything, let alone the play. *The Tempest* had remained for her the only small sparkle of light left in this whole sorry business. Now, it seemed, even *that* spark was to be extinguished.

'When the present redecoration of their dormitory is complete,' the voice went inexorably on, 'the girls from the Remove will return there from their temporary quarters. And so to the tour of the school.'

Alison let out a gasping sigh.

Mechanically the girls rose, filing line by line from their seats and tramping after their mentor up the stairs, along the passages and on towards the attics.

The building appeared suddenly to have turned into a prison. Miss Cowley sat on, slumped in her chair, long after the last row had departed. Finally she blinked back to life and, rising, walked to her study. She *presumed* she could still call it her study? Perhaps in a moment she would be enlightened about that too by the arrogant second mistress.

At the end of the line on the first landing, Alison and Sally were hanging back. Both girls' brows were creased with torment.

'Never was one for crocodiles,' Alison growled savagely.

'Nor me, old Aligator,' agreed her companion, with equal bitterness.

'So – what about an exeat?'

'Oh, you defiant temptress! You can't mean – to see Teddy?'

'I don't see why not,' Alison returned, throwing everything to the winds now. 'I'm sick to the teeth of this place.'

'Oh, but it's a super wheeze, old thing,' Sally assured. 'Only one snag. Who do we ask?'

The sparkling blue eyes were round with expectancy. For this was an entirely new Alison Dayne: a mutinous, disobedient and rebellious Alison Dayne.

'Why not the Head?' The rebel peered upward with infinite distaste, to where the lines of girls could still be heard tramping along the endless corridors above. 'There's still only one at St Ursula's, thank goodness.'

And of course it was true. Both girls knew they were going to back Miss Cowley to the hilt, to the very death if need be, in that battle for the survival of the fittest. It was without so much as a backward glance that Alison ran downstairs and knocked on the study door.

'Come in,' whispered a tired and fragile voice. They entered, quietly and respectfully. 'Yes, girls? What is it?' The temporary Headmistress sat facing them.

'Miss Cowley,' said Alison without hesitation. 'May we have an exeat?'

The mistress blinked. 'An exeat? But certainly . . .'

'And if there's anything we can get you while we're out . . .' Alison spoke so clearly and firmly that the Head involuntarily straightened and, taking a lace handkerchief from her pocket, blew her nose.

'I think not,' she said. 'But how *thoughtful*, nevertheless. Thankfully, in every school there are some persons one may instinctively trust.' The poor woman was unable to stop the crack in her voice. She had to rise and turn towards the window in order to wipe away the tear that refused to be held back any longer.

Alison looked at Sally, and vehemently that girl nodded. Taking fate in both her hands, Alison stepped forward.

'Miss Cowley,' she began huskily, 'we're shocked and cut to the quick to see Miss Prosser taking over like this.'

'Golly, yes,' Sally vigorously affirmed. 'Miss Devine would be furious to know the woman was back here again.'

Miss Cowley turned to the two girls in real sorrow.

'Unfortunately,' she murmured in her quiet voice, 'as it was the Governors' decision, there is nothing I can do. I know,' she added, 'that I have no right to be talking like this, but I cannot get over the fact that she has taken it upon herself to cancel my play rehearsals at Coxley Grange. Never was I so deliberately snubbed.' There followed a pause and a sniff. 'No. I am not a fit person to be in control of St Ursula's, and had much better resign.'

'Eh?' squeaked Sally. 'Oh corks!'

'Corks?'

'I mean you can't *do* that. Life'd be impossible here.' There came a longer pause, and then: 'Listen. I know I'm sticking my neck out like anything . . .'

'Well, come on,' Alison growled. 'Spit it out.'

'Hang on, Ali. Don't rush me. It's just that I'm having one of my brainstorms. I mean we all know Mr Forson and his funny ideas. If he's so besotted with *The Tempest*, why don't we get *him* working on Prosey, because . . . because, well,' she gasped eagerly, 'the play's the thing, after all.'

While the brilliance of the scheme sank in, Miss Cowley stared.

'Good Heavens.' It was worth a try. Anything was worth a try. Mechanically, she picked up the phone.

'But that's terrible, Miss Cowley,' came the clearly audible, rasping but infinitely reassuring tones of Mr Forson. 'The play most certainly *is* the thing. And you reckon I should try to sweeten the old dame up? Well, sure. We have Lord and Lady Logan coming to dine here this very evening. Maybe your Miss P would like to join the little party? I'll get on to her right away.'

'D'you think it'll work?' asked Sally as the phone went down again.

'I am not sure, my dear.' The mistress managed a wan smile. 'Since nothing in my life appears at this moment to be "working", I should say, probably not. It was nevertheless an excellent plan and I am most grateful. You will perhaps know that Miss Devine has been a friend of mine for years.' Miss Cowley gazed pensively through the window at a garden now emptied of life. 'I was at college with her mother, you see. I even wonder whether I ought to telegraph for her return to St Ursula's. These feelings are merely instinctive. Sally, is it not? It is perhaps unkind of me to suggest you may have imagined your monkish apparition – no, stay – I am not doubting your veracity. But might it not have been some tall wardrobe looming from the shadows? Perhaps you find it difficult to recall.' She paused. 'The grey lady on the other hand . . .'

'Yes?' Alison breathed.

'Kitty's grey lady is entirely another matter.'

'Oh golly, you think so, Miss Cowley? You can't imagine how relieved that makes me feel just now.'

'But indeed. Contrary to an earlier statement, I am a firm believer in such phenomena. There was an accuracy about the timing of the manifestation that we ignore at our peril.' The mistress sneezed once, then twice. Then she drifted slowly round the table. Her eyes had become fixed on the empty glass inkstand. With its host of small bubbles, the thing suddenly looked uncannily like some queer crystal ball. 'I see,' she murmured hypnotically, 'something inside this school that I do not like at all. I see . . . I see . . .' (Sally took hold of her friend's arm) 'I see danger ahead.' The mistress's eyes had begun to close. She looked in danger of dropping off.

'Yes? Yes?' Alison enquired urgently.

'I see an empty building.' Miss Cowley came to life again. 'The wind blows through its shattered windows. Its doors bang about in the storm. There is a great howling, a screaming of wind. And then a *collapse*.'

They waited.

'Collapse?'

'Yes. A great collapse.'

'And that's it? That's all?' Sally ventured tremulously at last.

The mistress sighed, as she shook her head despairingly.

'Is it not enough?' she asked, collapsing in her chair. 'Take your exeat. Go and amuse yourselves. And yes, there *is* after all something I would like you to buy for me – a small bottle of aspirins. I feel another cold coming on.'

An hour later, seated in her cousin's tiny room by the bow window, Alison was explaining the facts.

'So you see, Teddy, even if Sally and Jen's monk *was* only someone playing a stupid trick . . .'

She held a cup of tea in one hand and a slice of the most delicious currant cake completely neglected in the other. Although this was her first time ever at Teddy's cosy lodgings which looked out on to the steep cobbled street, the girl had no eyes for her surroundings and little appetite for the cake.

'. . . it doesn't make life any easier,' Sally explained, 'because they could play it again.'

'And again and again,' Alison insisted, noticing the cake and cramming it into her mouth, 'until the whole school ends up in chaos,' she added in muffled tones. 'And you know what that'll mean? Kitty and I'll be so unpopular with Prosey, life simply won't be worth living.'

'Oh, I *know* it wasn't a wardrobe,' Sally wailed.

'Right!' Teddy had come to a decision and pushed back his chair from the tiny round table. Everything in this house seemed to be minute, except Teddy himself. 'Why don't we all calm down,' he declared, 'and pop round to see Mrs Trimble?'

'Who's Mrs Trimble?' came two girlish voices in unison.

'Her husband's the gardener at Coxley Grange.'

'Ooh, er . . .' said Alison.

'She was the cook at St Ursula's when it was just plain Semley Hall.'

'*Semley Hall?*' Alison stuttered, almost choking over the last few crumbs of cake.

'Good Heavens,' Sally exclaimed. 'That was the name of that old book you were reading . . .'

'She only lives two doors away,' Teddy explained. 'If anyone knows about spooks there, she will.'

A moment later they were outside that country person's double doors listening to a weird tale.

'Well yes, sir, there *is* a spook as you call it.'

Sally looked up eagerly, most keen to have her story confirmed at last. For no-one, not even Alison herself, seemed to take it seriously any more, which was galling in the extreme.

'And a rare sight she be too . . .'

'You say *she*?' demanded Sally indignantly.

'Certainly.'

'No monk?' Teddy enquired.

'Oh no, sir, not a monk. She's a lonely, shadowy lady and 'tis said she guards a treasure what no-one 'as never found and . . .'

'*Kitty*'s ghost!'

'. . . and, 'tis said,' Miss Trimble went on, warming now to her theme, 'that when she appears there'll be a disaster in that house that won't be truly over till she's come once again.'

The lady leaned back in satisfaction. As though to give further weight to her words, she also nodded sagely.

'Good Heavens, so it's true,' exclaimed Teddy, passing a handkerchief over his brow. 'Trust that Kitty! Thanks, Mrs Trimble. You've been a brick. Here's a shilling for your trouble.'

'Oh please, sir. Nothing like that, sir. George wouldn't like it. I don't rightly remember *your* name now – just so as I can tell 'im when he comes home.'

'Dayne . . . Edward Dayne.'

'Dayne,' said the plump lady, troubled. 'There now, that '*as* got a familar ring, though I'm blessed where I've heard it before . . .'

An unusual conversation was going on next morning inside the main porch at St Ursula's School for Girls. It was taking place between the Headmistress, Miss Cowley, and the second mistress, Miss Prosser.

How lucky that Verity Lamton had been within earshot from its very beginning. Otherwise she might have missed something. And that would have been a pity. Because, in this exchange, the previous roles of the two mistresses were entirely and most inexplicably reversed.

While Miss Cowley rapped out sarcasms, it was Miss Prosser's turn, apparently, to creep and crawl – or so it appeared to Verity. Had she not heard for herself, she would never have believed it possible. Neither mistress paid any attention to the hopping, bird-like figure beside the notice-board. Miss Prosser had just pinned a notice there, and what are notices for, if not to be read? Verity, of less than average height, almost strained her neck trying to read it. She could have saved herself the trouble.

'Ah! Miss Cowley,' cried the second mistress. 'Just the person I wanted to see!'

To that simpering tone, Verity Lamton was not the only astonished listener. Miss Cowley could not believe her ears either.

'I have some good news for you,' the mistress rattled on. 'I was at dinner last night with Lord and Lady Logan, you know . . .' The voice became here very roguish.

'Oh yes?' Miss Cowley replied coldly, since this other person was evidently waiting for some reaction to what, for herself at any rate, seemed to have been a satisfying occasion.

'I really tried my utmost to reverse Mr Forson's decision not to allow the girls into his grounds for the play.'

'*Mr Forson*'s decision?

This time Miss Cowley really did react. She almost said 'Pah!' But if there was anything in her manner to suggest such a curt dismissal, Miss Prosser did not appear to notice. The skin of the second mistress was made of some fibrous material. Canvas would possibly describe it. Quite unruffled, she continued:

'Yes, and I am gratified to be able to report that I entirely succeeded. The rehearsals are to go ahead as planned.'

Now Miss Cowley truly exploded.

'Really?' she roared, her ample bosom swelling like a turkey cock's.

'Yes,' smiled the other. 'Really.'

There came a momentary stupefied pause while Miss Cowley struggled with some deep inner emotion. Then at last the temporary Head gave voice.

'Miss Prosser,' she burst out. 'I don't know what sort of reaction you were expecting. I admit mine is one of disbelief. That, as a former mistress, you feel able simply to sweep back into this school and make whatever decisions you like, completely over my head – that is something *quite* outside my experience. I have lost my enthusiasm for *The Tempest*, Miss Prosser, and there are matters to which I must attend.'

She turned on her heel and, in a flurry of clothing, left. Miss Prosser, hastening after her Headmistress, barred the way.

'You have taken offence,' she explained kindly, 'because of something inadvertently uttered by myself. I cannot think what it was but let me make my full apology now. Let me assure you, there was no malign intent whatever.'

'Miss Prosser,' Miss Cowley shot back at her, 'there is no need to defer in quite such an unctuous manner!'

'Then I am forgiven? The play is to proceed at Coxley Grange as planned?'

There was just a hint of a frosty glance here, directed at Verity, as Miss Prosser noticed the girl's presence in their midst for the first time. Verity deemed it wise to move, and did so just as Miss Cowley made her final utterance.

'If that is our joint wish.'

'It is, Miss Cowley. Indeed it is.'

Verity raced away to impart the news.

'Hang on a mo!' She fairly gasped out the words to the first ordinary human she spotted. This happened to be Tryphena Hargreaves.

'Yes?' answered Tryphena, without a great deal of interest. 'What is it, Verity - an apoplectic fit or merely a mild embolism?'

'Neither, actually. Have you heard the latest on Coxley's? No. I can see you haven't.'

Even Alison, in the library, could hear the piercing, squeaky voice and now, here was Tryphena excitedly relaying the news to Sally.

'Did you ever hear anything so ridic? First Prosey completely bans Coxley Grange - makes it out of bounds to everyone - then suddenly it's all changed and we're totally back to normal. I find it quite hilarious, I must say! Got to go and find Avelyne.'

Sally shoved her head round the door with a triumphant smirk.

'Hear all that? He's certainly got a way with him, our Mr Forson!'

Of course, Sally had engineered it all. And that was satisfying to know. But Alison, mysteriously enough, gained less satisfaction from the revelation than had her friends. No lover of Coxley's, it had also puzzled her to imagine what must have been said by the astonishing American to effect such a dramatic turn-about.

Unlike Sally Spencer, Miss Prosser was not an easily seducable person, and the aristocracy were well known to leave her as cold as a dead flatfish. For a moment, the girl's heart lifted. Supposing Mr Forson or the Logan chap had offered Prosey another job? Hadn't the woman been a governess at one time? Perhaps the noble Lord had suggested an astronomical sum, if only she would take on the education of some ghastly offspring who needed thoroughly putting down?

On Miss Devine's return, certainly, Miss Prosser's appointment would have to terminate. Alison's brows knitted. She'd taken in every word of Mrs Trimble's cryptic warnings. Now, in her further perusal of *The Legends and History of Semley Hall*, the girl had come across a passage which added an entirely new dimension to those utterances. Alison at that moment determined to embark on a series of investigations in the school.

They would not be easy. Since they involved a comprehensive search of the whole building, they promised, on the contrary, to be infinitely protracted. But until she found what she sought, the girl had at last realized, no-one at St Ursula's could rest easily in their beds . . . those of them, at any rate, who were left.

No painting or other form of decoration had taken place in Primrose Dormitory, certainly. The room stood as empty and forlorn as the day they'd left it. Indeed, the members of both the other Remove dormies were being told at that very moment to pack and head for Coxley's – for the sake of convenience, according to Miss Prosser.

Everyone had envied the girls of Primrose dorm. Nothing could be more attractive than this room in the big house. The birds sang under the eaves. The wall creeper peeped in at the windows. The beds were soft and the carpet admirable for waggling your toes in on the way to the luxurious bathroom. Yet Alison fretted.

She occasionally went up and sat in the old Primrose, imagining Jen and Hil there with her still.

As the days went by, an unruffled calm now settled on the

old school. It settled because, during leisure hours at any rate, hardly anyone seemed to be there. They were all down the road, disporting themselves on the tennis courts, or fooling around on the lawn, or inside the house, or just messing about in boats – well, at least, one particular kind of boat.

With the *Tempest* rehearsals thoroughly under way, Mr Forson's raft attracted them like a magnet. Large, and painted red, it possessed rails, and a ship's light, and even a kind of poopdeck. But above all it had a wonderful sail, that in catching the wind would set the ponderous craft in motion. Slowly and infinitely satisfyingly, it moved across the placid waters of the lake, to the accompaniment of delighted screams.

Everyone wanted to be on the capacious raft at once, including the girls who were not even in the play, and in particular those intrepid first years whose idea *The Tempest* had originally been.

'Oh, I do so wish you hadn't made it at all, Mr Forson,' Miss Cowley moaned, wringing her hands for the fifth time that afternoon. The raft was at that moment bulging with budding actresses, all squealing at once. They were rollicking girls, who clung to the mast and leaned over the sides dangling their hands and looking at their own beautiful reflections in the water. The American's voice purred in reply.

'It's a fine craft, dear lady, made with my own delicate hands.'

'I know. But we never seem to do any actual rehearsing. We've been at the thing a fortnight and we're no nearer than when we started. Come on now!' she cried hoarsely, clapping her hands for silence. 'Will you please pull yourselves together, girls, or it'll be chaos on the night. Tryphena?'

'Ah . . . Mmm. Let me see,' Tryphena obliged, flicking over the pages of the set book. 'Here we are. "Master? What cheer? Speak to the mariners. Fall t'it yarely, or we run ourselves aground."'

'Actually,' squeaked someone, 'we *are* aground – not moving, anyway. Give us a shove, Mabel.'

Mr Forson, fingers itching as always, could no longer resist.

'Heave to, little girl,' the fat man roared, springing from the bridge in a mighty leap that set the raft a-drifting for all it was worth. '"Heigh, my hearts!"' he yelled above the storm. '"Cheerly, cheerly my hearts. Yare. Yare. Take in the top-sail . . .!"'

Someone obliged. The heavy canvas collapsed on his head. Miss Cowley glanced upward. Thinking of storms, a black cloud had indeed momentarily shut out the warmth of the sun. She peered helplessly back at the raft. Under that heaving topsail (also made by his own fair hands) Mr Forson was now struggling ineffectually.

'"Tend to the Master's whistle,"' came his muffled voice.

'Whistle, someone!' Miss Cowley sang out the command in a crisp sharp tone. The task had been generously given to the very smallest girl – one Letitia. 'I said whistle!'

The whistle blew faintly.

'"Blow till thou burst thy wind if room enough,"' sighed the real bosun, in the absence of any further response from under the sail to that faint trill. 'Oh glory. We're drifting *right* away from the shore.'

'I say!' called the Master. 'Where's the oar, actually?'

'"Good Bosun have care,"' shrieked Alonso. '"Where's the Master? Play the . . . play the men . . . "' The child almost collapsed over the side. 'I'm sorry Miss Cowley. I really can't manage to say that line. It's too ridiculous.'

'Antonio?' Miss Cowley shouted.

The sun still had not reappeared. The angry black cloud was, if anything, getting bigger. It threatened rain, and for a moment Miss Cowley's spirits lifted.

'Oh yes,' answered Antonio, emerging from the canvas. 'Er. "Where is the Master-bosun?" I mean . . . "where is the Master, Bosun?"'

'Stuck under this darn sail,' ground the American's plaintive voice. 'Can't someone get me outa here?'

'Oh, Mr Forson,' Miss Cowley wailed. 'We've got to do better than this.' Again she looked at that menacing sky. 'It's the dress rehearsal the day after tomorrow.'

A play of storms she had promised them, and a play of storms it suddenly seemed likely to be.

The mistress had long ago given up believing in this particular play by the well known playwright William Shakespeare and, in particular, in its outdoor performance. All attempts to communicate these doubts to Mr Forson, however, were like chaff thrown into a high wind. They were words cast to a force ten; and as she glanced first at Miss Prosser standing over there grinning like a black scarecrow, and then back at the sky, Miss Cowley finally admitted a hope – a trust, even – that it would rain on the night.

Indeed, she now expressed a devout new prayer. It was for a downpour that would begin immediately and last the whole of the next two days. Why couldn't that gloating ape of a woman take herself off and do handstands in the bushes? That smirking face had unnerved Miss Cowley completely. The old cat should not be allowed to win, no – not this time. In accordance with the contingency plan she had secretly devised, Miss Cowley transferred her mind, not this time to the fruit farm in Kent, but to the reassuring shelter of the school hall.

In that same school hall, three persons at this moment had the place to themselves. Around the abandoned buildings, there brooded an almost deathly quiet.

'Where *is* Alison?' Verity was snapping fractiously to Sally as they peered around in the gloom. Just when she'd managed to pin them both down to come and watch her performance in the play rehearsal, here was one of them suddenly escaped again. Alison in particular was like a slippery eel these days. There one minute, gone the next. 'Alison?' she called peevishly. 'Can you hear me?'

Reply came there none. The budding actress headed up the back stairs.

'Ali?' said Sally.

'I'm here,' came a quiet voice from aloft.

'Where?'

'On the main landing. Can you come up?'

'No, she can not,' came Verity's voice unnervingly from right beside her, making Alison jump. 'Some sort of weak joke at my expense, I assume. And why are you holding that mirror? I know you're conceited, but surely not *that* vain? There's a time and a place for looking in mirrors . . .'

With a last wistful look at the portrait hanging at the top of the stairs, Alison slipped the glass back into her pocket. As she followed the slim figure downstairs she did not venture a reply. Fortunately, Verity did not require one. There was actually no vanity left over for anybody else. Verity had collared all of it. The heroine was already late for rehearsal. Now Alison was making her even later.

For the fact that Alison's disappearance had derived from a sudden flash of inspiration meant little to either Sally or the Remove's shining light. Yet it was a token of her increasing trust in Sally Spencer that after briefly gazing at the picture, Alison's reaction had been impulsively to call her friend. It had been the exotic green jewel round the neck of the lady in the portrait which she had wished to discuss. Now caution held her back.

The rest of the features she had cleaned earlier. It only needed the mirror, now, to confirm what had been fermenting there in the back of her mind for several days. That the face so closely resembled her own was not the main point at issue. Mrs Trimble had spoken of a treasure. She had also told of a ghost. That pendant . . .

'Since you're supposed to be playing Miranda,' Sally laughed as they pushed open the main door and strode out into the open air, '. . . the only girl in the whole stupid production, Verity, I'm surprised you're not over there already.'

'Good gracious,' the other girl trilled in return. 'Stars don't sit around on wet grass.'

She glanced up at the dark heavens; at the lowering beetling cloud inside which, no doubt, the first drops were preparing themselves for descent to the earth, and gave it an answering glare.

Verity Lamton was keener on projecting her hitherto heavily under-rated image than she cared at this moment to admit. And it would be just typical to be foiled right at the last moment, by nothing more or less than the English weather. Here below hung a warm unnatural calm – up there, a heavy gathering, as though the Gods were assembling to pass judgement upon this paltry and earthbound reproduction of their own magic arts.

'What's the betting it'll rain on the night?' Verity uttered her most theatrical laugh. 'Just imagine – we could end up doing the whole thing in macintoshes!'

After all that preparation, it was certainly enough to make a hyena cry. And as if by way of response, as Sally held forth her hand, a single large drop splashed down into the oustretched palm.

'*Was* that rain?' Verity demanded indignantly.

''Fraid so, old prima donna.'

'Then I'm simply not going.'

The girl spun round. Then she stopped dead in her tracks and uttered a piercing scream.

'What the thump . . . ?'

'It was there, I tell you!' Verity goggled. 'Up on the roof.'

'What was?'

'The ghost.'

'I see no ghost.'

'No – because it ain't there any longer.'

'Then where is it?'

'How the heck do I know?'

Whatever, if anything, *had* been there, Verity turned and raced off in the opposite direction as fast as her legs would carry her. Sally only needed to look at Alison once for the briefest of silent communications. Then the two turned like greased lightning. In seconds they were back in the school.

At the bottom of the main staircase, Alison put a finger on her lips. They crept up the old oak boards two creaking steps at a time. On the landing Alison barely paused. The cold eyes of her own ancestor stared impassively down.

Instead, she kept on, up the second flight. These upper regions, too, seemed to be frowning, as if resenting such an untimely intrusion upon their melancholy.

'It wouldn't be here, would it?' Sally whispered doubtfully, keeping close to her friend. The senior dorms lay around them, as dark and still as death.

'It'll be in the attics . . .'

Oh crikey! *What* for goodness sake would be in the attics? Alison sounded so sure, and Sally did not relish another glimpse of the horrid thing she'd already seen once. There was no turning back. Alison was already mounting that narrow stairway of unpolished wood.

Slowly, cautiously, Alison peered round the doorway at the top. Save for empty trunks piled from floor to ceiling, there was nothing of interest. Sally followed into the increasing gloom, rounded a corner and then suddenly stopped.

Rain pattered on the slates above. There was a light ahead. A shaft of dusty light came from the window that led out on to the roof. The casement was open.

Alison swung her leg over the dusty sill on to the wet parapet. Sally preferred to keep off those dizzy heights. So anxiously was she watching for her friend's safety, in fact, that she did not even hear the footsteps . . .

'Come back, Ali,' she hissed.

There *was* nothing to see on the roofs, nor out across the park save green grass and the American, presumably still declaiming out there beyond the marshy ground that separated the school from his lake and grand domain. So Alison returned as she was bid, climbing back into the arms of . . . a tall thin figure clutching a long pointed knife!

Even if you ignored the bowler hat altogether, the man before Sally and Alison presented an unusual appearance. Over more conventional clothes he wore a long grey hooded garment, liberally festooned with cobwebs.

'D'you *have* to creep up on people like that?' squeaked Alison.

'Sorry, Miss. But I didn't want to frighten you.'

'You scared me out of my rotten wits! Why are you wearing that ridiculous get up? And what on *earth* are you waving that knife for?'

'I'm a surveyor, Miss. I'm proddin' these here timbers for signs of wet rot, dry rot and the much affeared death watch beetle. If it's of any interest, I can tell you this place has got the lot.' He jabbed a beam, producing a cloud of dust. 'And I shouldn't jump about quite so blithely on them boards, or you'll be deposited in the classroom below.'

He had a curious manner of speaking; more like a policeman, somehow, then a surveyor of property.

'It isn't a classroom,' Sally snapped. 'It's a fifth form dormitory and - oh, botheration! We could have been at the play thing watching Verity getting soaked, if it hadn't been for you scrabbling about on the roof.'

'I am only doing my duty, Miss.'

'Now where *is* Verity?' Miss Cowley was fretting, back at that same play. The rain splashed steadily, but still gently, making beautiful circles in the lake's calm surface. Apart from the rain there was only one other trouble with this particular set book, and that was Mr Forson.

Except for that of the absent Miranda, he could and presumably would play *all* the roles. The fact that Miranda was the only real girl in this otherwise all 'male' cast, was a disadvantage Miss Cowley had to admit she had *not* foreseen.

At this moment the American was prodding a prone and hidden Caliban with his foot.

'"What have we here? A man or a fish? Dead or alive? A fish: he smells like a fish; a very ancient and fishlike smell; a kind of not-of-the-newest Poor John. A strange fish!"' the man droned on inexorably. '"Were I in England now, as once I was, and had but this fish painted, not a holiday fool there but would give a piece of silver."' The actor, thankfully, forgot a couple of lines. "'Alas,'" he moaned, '"the storm is come again: my best way is to creep under his gaberdine. There is no other shelter hereabout: misery acquaints a man with strange bedfellows."'

There came a screech from Caliban and then a loud clap of thunder. The rain suddenly began to tip down. Mr Forson climbed under the 'gaberdine', in reality a school raincoat. Caliban climbed out.

'Your macs, girls,' Miss Cowley screeched, 'and to the shelter of the Colonnade!'

A mass scramble took place to that outside portion of the house selected by Mr Forson as shelter in case of storms at sea. In fact, his disappointment at having to stop acting for a moment was almost completely appeased by this opportunity to put into practice another of his good ideas.

As the jostling, chattering bodies crowded under the arched stone gallery that projected coveniently from a back wing of the Grange, Miss Cowley took her courage in both hands.

'I am afraid, Mr Forson, we cannot risk this happening on the night. I fear we shall simply have to transfer the dress rehearsal and the performances themselves over to the school.'

'Aw . . .' The American peered outside again. 'You've spoiled things, darn you!' he frowned, wagging an accusing finger at the rain. 'Couldn't we do it in *this* house maybe? I gotta lovely big room.'

'I do *love* it here, Miss Cowley,' Monica Hargreaves affirmed. 'If St Ursula's ever had to be anywhere else . . . this is where I'd like it . . .'

'Somewhere else?' Miss Cowley gaped. The idea had never occurred to her.

'There's no chance of that, I hope,' Philippa Treadway retorted.

'What d'you mean, you hope?'

'I mean I *hope*, Monica, you goofy clown,' that girl was warmly informed. 'Because St Ursula's is St Ursula's. I have feelings for the old school, even if you haven't.'

'Yes,' came several voices in support. 'St Ursula's for ever!'

Mr Forson had taken his cigar out of his mouth. Now he replaced it thoughtfully as, cheeks red and nose dripping with water, he glared across the soggy expanse of lawn. He spoke with new glumness.

'OK – You're right, I guess,' he said. 'We'd better do it in your hall. It's your play, girls.' He sighed. 'I don't know why I'm so bothered – I ain't even in the darn thing.' His tone was soul searching, reduced to sadness by those dreams of an arcadia now vanished. Then he brightened. 'Still, you do have a gallery over there, if I remember. I reckon that's what the Bard would'a used, eh? I'm going to get a drink. I don't know about you, Miss Cowley, but my throat's real parched.'

'I'm not surprised,' the mistress could not help replying as she watched the plump figure waddle away through the descending drops and in at the nearest door.

'Look,' remarked Tryphena Hargreaves. 'Here come two persons on bicyles. Whoever can they be?'

'One of them's Verity Lamton,' Monica replied. 'I can't quite make out the other . . . Why! I do declare it's Miss Prosser.'

And Miss Prosser it was.

A general groan went through the steaming company. Miss Cowley gulped.

'More trouble,' she muttered, her voice trailing away as, followed by a scowling Verity, the figure in the voluminous black cycling cape came labouring round the corner of the house.

'Miss Cowley! Do I find you at last?'

As she dropped her machine to glare at the assembled players, the fact that this was a true enquiry rather than Miss Prosser's customary command became clearer.

Presumably as a result of her unaccustomed exertion, the mistress's spectacles were completely steamed up. She could see, perhaps, the odd head poking around the sides of the general mist, but otherwise no more than a blur of people.

Those glasses served rather to hinder than assist any view of the desired Miss Cowley. Yet so great was Prosser's exhaustion that she seemed prepared to assume the temporary Head's presence among the throng, and launched into the latest bulletin.

'Miss Cowley . . .' she began, scraggy chest heaving, 'we are in trouble again, I fear. It concerns *this* poor child,' she explained, gathering Verity protectively into the unpleasant clammy folds of her glistening wet cloak, 'a perfectly reliable girl from the Remove form.'

The perfectly reliable Removite looked up indignantly, only to receive a stream of water in her face as the mistress looked down. A small reservoir had collected in the rim of the sou' wester. Now Verity got it straight in the eye. With a yell of indignation, she tried to struggle free, but to no avail. The mistress had a grip like a pair of pliers.

'Ah, Mr Forson! You too will be interested in this, I think.' She had at last remembered to remove her specs.

Just emerging with drinks for everyone, the startled benefactor all but dropped the tray. He glanced longingly backwards. Miss Prosser, however, possessed a quality of command sufficient to unnerve a battery, and she was just getting into her stride.

'This girl,' she continued evenly after a pause of suitable length, 'was walking along perfectly quietly, when she turned to descry another vile apparition – this time upon the school roof! Is that not correct?'

'Yes,' sulked Verity, removing the last traces of water from her eye.

'Was it motionless or moving?'

'Both.'

'And with wings, you said, did you not? Black wings?'

'I can't be sure of the colour,' Verity growled.

'And a forked tail, no doubt.' Mr Forson had finally pulled himself together. 'Oh cheese it, Prosser. We're quite busy here with a play.'

'Mr Forson, really!'

Verity escaped the encircling arms at last and returned to the flock, amongst which, extremely put out, she hid herself and disappeared.

'How terrifying,' Miss Cowley found herself gasping, in spite of all saner convictions.

'It is more than terrifying. It is outrageous, and shows that St Ursula's is no longer a fit home for the children of fee paying parents. Action must be delayed no longer. When is the dress rehearsal?'

'The day after tomorrow,' Miss Cowley replied weakly.

'Then may I suggest an immediate meeting with Major Farquhar? Say, tomorrow at three o'clock?'

It was at this moment that a sodden Alison and Sally chose to make their appearance on the scene. After sheltering under a tree for some time on their way over to the play rehearsal, they had eventually given up all hope of either sun or dramatic entertainment. Yet here the latter was in plenty.

'Oh shucks, why?' Mr Forson was grumbling as Miss Cowley bristled.

'I should have thought that perfectly obvious,' retorted Prosser, in a tone of singular insolence. 'To seek some remedy for a haunting - a ghost if you will - that threatens the very existence of our school. One first witnessed' (noticing the new arrivals she was able with a shudder to add emphatically) 'by none other than the irrepressible cousin of our own Alison Dayne!'

'Why cannot those girls be quiet? Quiet, you girls!'

The meeting had begun, and Miss Prosser was in good voice.

After that snap decision to stage the dress rehearsal inside the St Ursula's hall, preparations for the performance the following evening had been going on most of the morning.

It was so irritating to Miss Cowley to have been interrupted in these preparations, that for once she'd actually put her foot down about something. The meeting would not, at any rate, take place in *her* study. That room was too full of play 'props'. There was a stage to be erected; with hastily contrived decorations. There were flowers to be arranged everywhere; curtains to be hung – not to mention the high wire.

The notion that Ariel should actually fly had been another of Mr Forson's spectacular inspirations. It was perhaps because of such worries, indeed, that the first years' classroom, into which the meeting had been relegated, reeked of cigar smoke.

As Miss Cowley watched, the American paced the room, puffing furiously. He seemed to be pondering something; whether the high wire his fingers evidently itched to put up, or some other deeper concern, she could not tell.

Mr Forson's frustration, indeed, seemed even deeper than that of the red faced, irritable looking Major who sat alone at the table, impatiently clasping his hands. The Chairman of the Governors could certainly see little justification for this sudden meeting of Prosser's. Apart from this extremely dubious roof affair, there had been no other ghostly manifestations for the whole of the last fortnight!

What worried the Major much more was the way things had been disappearing from the school. Somebody had been turning the place upside down and, in the process, removing the odd clock here, the odd vase there. Nothing of any real value had been taken, luckily. That was the peculiar thing. It was as though the person were searching for some special object he could not locate.

Anyway, the Major had been in contact with the local police force. There was little else he *could* do in the circumstances. With all this ghost nonsense hanging in the air one had to be careful, or the children would become even more upset. Faced with the task of running the place in the absence of Miss Devine, the simple minded military man found the whole affair deeply annoying. He wished some simple solution might appear from the heavens.

It was tactless of Miss Prosser to have brought up the ghost nonsense again, just when he thought that *that*, at least, had quietened down. Still, he would take this opportunity of bringing up in turn the matter of the thieving. Perhaps Forson might have some good ideas.

There were indeed many possible explanations for the thing on the roof. Major Farquhar had told her so. The second mistress, however, seemed perversely anxious not to know what either Alison or Sally Spencer could have confirmed, had they arrived a few moments earlier at the Colonnade. How unfortunate, therefore, that they had not done so . . .

For neither Alison nor Sally had felt in any hurry to get to Coxley Grange that afternoon, in spite of the rain. They had walked along talking of unimportant things. It was a stupid situation. Each girl had something she wished to say to the other. Neither girl felt able to gasp it out. When Alison impulsively called up the stairs to Sally, it had been because she had felt a sudden urge to communicate with this new friend whom, every day, she grew to like more and more. She had wanted to share the discovery she had made about one of her ancestors. Then Verity had barged in and spoiled things as usual, and the old familiar Dayne caution had reasserted itself.

After that, Alison had found herself deliberately steering the conversation away from grey ladies and their mysterious jewellery. For was this not the 'other reason' why Colonel Dayne had chosen St Ursula's as her school. Who knew *what* extra secret motives her father might have had? He had refused to tell her himself. The knowledge might spoil her relationship with the other girls. Sally was 'another girl' and Alison considered herself no snob. She wouldn't even, on reflection, have told Hil and Jen. Teddy was another matter. Teddy was family.

Great minds think alike. Sally was also absorbed in thoughts of Teddy on that wet ambling walk under the new green leaves. She was too busy with them even to have considered why Alison had called her upstairs.

For Sally had lost much of that old carefree manner. It *was* true that on the day of the tea party in the study she had asked Jennifer to pop off, so she could have a clear field with these Daynes. But not Teddy alone. She had also wanted Alison to herself for a change, and Jennifer had known it.

Sally was a person who needed reassurance. She badly needed it now. Jen had still not returned to St Ursula's, even though her injuries had apparently almost cleared up. Just suppose she *never* came back? Suppose her parents decided to send her to some other school?

Sally felt it would be a judgement. Things *had* been beastly since that rotten fall. She had tried to communicate her feelings. Indeed, she was always trying to chat to Alison. But to 'chatter' Alison singularly failed to respond.

So Miss Spencer wanted someone else to whom she could confess her guilt. She felt sure she could explain to Teddy what she could never convey to Alison, that if she *had* been trying to flirt a little, at least now she bitterly regretted it. Then he would reassure and comfort her; and everything would be all right. Jennifer would come back. St Ursula's would somehow revert to its cheerful self again, all ready for Miss Devine's triumphal return. Sadly, she could *never* see Teddy alone. So Sally was back where she started. There remained between the two girls this unnerving self-consciousness, which neither knew how to put into words. It was curious, as though some third force were deliberately trying to keep them apart.

An odd thing for a long dead ancestor to want to do? Maybe. But then, everything in this school was getting stranger and stranger.

This meeting, for instance; nothing could be more strange than the reason Miss Prosser had advanced for it: 'a solution to a haunting'. *Could* there be such a solution? Ghosts don't take to being bossed around. If there *was* an answer, Alison wanted to hear.

'Mr Forson,' Miss Prosser was patiently explaining, 'I am simply trying to suggest an answer to what, as you must realize, has become a most frightful problem.'

Did he realize? It was difficult to tell. The room was now so thick with cigar smoke that, after an expression of disgust, the second mistress crossed over to the window and flung it open.

The American seemed suddenly to make up his mind about something, and stopped his pacing about.

'All right, tell us this suggestion,' he demanded.

'Only that, because of the disruptive elements currently disturbing our lives at St Ursula's, I wondered if you might find us some more dormitory space?'

'Well, I could,' frowned the cigar chewing millionaire, with a twist of the cheek. 'But I reckon I've worked out a better plan.' He looked up, drew in his breath, then stared the Chairman of the Governors straight in the eye. 'Why don't you move the whole school to Coxley Grange – lock, stock and barrel, classrooms, everything. There. I've said it.'

Miss Cowley had been dozing in a desk very much too small for her. Now she sprang to her feet and nearly broke a femur.

'What?' she gasped. 'What then will *you* do?'

'Simple. I take up residence here.'

Mr Forson grinned and rubbed his hands. He appeared suddenly to be enjoying *this* drama just as much as the other. The Major was spluttering, while the dismay of the acting Head was plain for all to see. Only Miss Prosser seemed undismayed. In fact, a quivering excitement had been allowed to break through on her normally mask-like face.

Major Farquhar came at last to life, exploding after the delayed reaction.

'You can't be serious!'

'I've never been *more* serious! Major, I came to your country to find my ancestral home.' Mr Forson was now thoroughly warming to his new role. 'Many years ago, generations of my family occupied this very house. Here the name of Forson was revered.'

At this point the cupboard door actually opened a fraction and the white face of Alison Dayne peeped, unseen, out of the narrow gap. There *must* be some mistake . . .

Alison had read a good deal about Semley Hall during the last couple of weeks. Daynes had been there in plenty. But never once in that large tome devoted to its legends and history, had she seen any mention of Forsons. Yet the American seemed completely convinced of his claim as, cigar puffing furiously, he paced around the blackboard.

'You see, Major,' he continued, in a voice of the deepest drama, 'I believe these ghosts of yours to be none other than the spirits of my own family dead, rising from their vaults to clamour for the return of a noo Forson.'

It was an astonishing assertion. Major Farquhar made a last effort to pull himself together.

'A romantic notion, sir,' he winced. 'But could we revert for a moment to practicality? I mean – How would you propose the move took place?'

'Why Major,' the American laughed, 'a straight swap. I can't offer better than that. Could be the bargain of the year, I guess. Coxley's is in much better shape. The grounds are superior. The sporting facilities are fantastic! I've been very happy there but, I can assure you all, my heart is right here; ghosts or no ghosts – and I mean it!'

'Miss Devine will never consent to any of this,' Miss Cowley bayed like a bloodhound. 'It's a nightmare.' Surely anyone in their right mind could see *that*? The military man, however, disillusioned her.

'I fear it has little to do with Miss Devine,' he observed unhappily. 'If the Governors decide to accept – and I must say, I think they very well might – there can be little doubt that we shall be taking advantage of what can only be seen as an outstandingly generous offer and a wonderful opportunity for the school. I have just seen a report from my surveyor on the condition of the roof. It seems the necessary repairs are likely to run into thousands of pounds. If Miss Devine *did* refuse to agree . . .' and here the red faced gentleman noisily cleared his throat '. . . well, then I am afraid there would have to be a *new* Headmistress.' Almost automatically, he glanced at Miss Prosser.

Her worst fears confirmed, the deputy Head also turned to that gloating face.

'Well!' she exploded. 'I might have known it!'

The second mistress seemed rather more confused by the accusatory glare from her colleague than one might have expected. She appeared to be searching for some suitably conciliatory gesture, in fact.

'To avoid, er . . . possible recriminations later on,' she smiled, baring her teeth unpleasantly, 'I ought, perhaps, to make the following suggestion.'

'Well, go on!' the Major snapped.

'Simply this. Giving due consideration to the gravity of the circumstances, should we perhaps not be *too* hasty in our conclusion of this affair? Ought our horrid phantom, the blight of our school . . . not be given one last chance to show its hand?'

'Eh?' the Major said, after a silence. He peered at Mr Forson for enlightenment. The American seemed content merely to rub his chin. 'Well, I must say . . .' the Chairman said (for want of anything better). 'That is very *singular* Miss Prosser. I take your point, I suppose; but then, let contracts be exchanged with all speed!' He laughed harshly. 'Or Mr Forson might be tempted to change his mind, eh? That would never do.' He laughed again. 'Ha, ha. How very bizarre.' What was the matter with the woman? Hadn't she got what she wanted? 'Miss Devine, of course,' he added as an afterthought, 'will have to be informed.'

'*Informed*?' Miss Cowley managed to cry out, coming at last to the end of her tether. 'Merely informed? Is this the way you intend to run your new school? Because if it is, then I certainly wish for no part in the sordid affair. After tomorrow night's rehearsal of our play, I resign – something which I am sure will cause little or no distress to anyone, least of all my colleague here on the right.'

And bursting into tears, the foiled Head rushed from the room.

The weather, so threatening during these past few days, had broken at last and now raged around the high walls of the old school in a real storm.

Like a banshee, the wind howled; spiralling up, up through the twisted chimneys and deserted halls of St Ursula's School for Girls; twisting the weathercock back and forth, till it seemed it must be torn from its moorings on the roof.

The rain battered the casements. Flashing lightning lit up the rows of empty beds in Primrose Dorm, while thunder rumbled ominously.

But it was not simply because of the storm that Alison tossed so in her little bed. After listening to what had been said at that disgraceful meeting, she indeed doubted whether she would ever be able to sleep again.

As if wanting to clasp the dear old place to her bosom and keep it safe for Miss Devine, the girl had not left St Ursula's all day. Telling only Sally of her intention, she had crept up the back stairs at bedtime, to the old Primrose Dormitory, and now lay there alone with her imaginings.

One particular vision tormented this, the most loyal girl in the school, as she lay there in the darkness. It was the vision of Miss Devine returning to the emptied house – to broken windows and tattered curtains; and a merciless wind that howled through the deserted, mildewy halls and passages, just as it was doing now.

Oh, it was too awful! And trust Prosey to make such a stupid suggestion, as though *that* were going to somehow mitigate her crime. Giving the horrid blight one more last chance to show its hand, indeed! What an idea. Alison Dayne, like Miss Cowley, would never dream of entering any school which had Prosser as its Head.

Real or unreal, jape or no jape, the ghost might come again at any moment, with the second mistress probably helping it along. In fact, as the ghastly apparition hadn't deigned to make another appearance since Jen's accident, that time could be any moment now. Come to think of it, the last manifestation had been in here! Alison pulled the covers right up over her eyes. Try as she might, she could not shut out that awesome wind. From way down in the bowels of the building came an incessant banging sound. Was the place *already* empty? Had there ever been a school here at all, or was she back in Semley Hall, alone with the grey lady?

She'd never sleep, not with that enigmatic passage from *The Legends and History of Semley Hall* going through her mind like a musical refrain. She repeated the words aloud in a hollow and dismal voice:

'. . . Of uncertain value, the Talisman nevertheless remained under lock and key, untouched in its secret position, until the time of the wicked Sir Henry. Maddened by gambling debts, the impoverished baronet sought to remove and sell the piece. But so great by all accounts were the disturbances then created by certain unnamed spectres of the dead – many about the house being stricken through injury or other misfortune – that within a week the treasure had been returned to its former place.'

It was this elusive treasure that a similarly elusive Alison had sought during those frequent, annoying excursions away from Sally Spencer. Instinctively, her footsteps always led her to that face on the landing, whose uncanny resemblance to her own now served simply to confirm what she had always inwardly realized.

If the necklace was this 'Talisman', the 'treasure' to which Mrs Trimble had referred, then must not there also be in the portrait some clue as to its hiding place within the school? The Talisman had to be the focus of all this malignant activity.

If the treasure had been moved, say by mice, even, or had somehow slipped down one of those new, alarming cracks in the foundations, then until it had been replaced the curse of the grey lady and all her attendant demons would go on, bringing St Ursula's finally to its knees. A persistent banging, which had been jarring her nerves for some time, finally demanded her full attention. Oh, how frustrating everything was. She would have to go down and shut that wretched door before it drove her mad.

In her subconscious, Alison realized, she had been waiting for someone else to perform the unsavoury task. Doubtless, no one dared. Well, *she* wasn't scared. Let nobody call Alison Dayne a funk. In fact, she was glad of an excuse to get out of this dreadful room.

Swinging her long legs from the bed, she first rummaged for, then found, her trusty torch. Then she padded out into the passage, flopped down the narrow stairs and emerged, cautiously peering round, into the shadows of the empty hall.

Here, *everything* creaked. Pieces of scenery ready for tomorrow's *Tempest* rehearsal flapped unnervingly, while from the gallery came a high pitched whining, like the wind in telephone cables.

A trapeze expert from London had been hired at great expense by the American to erect the wire for Ariel's flying act. If Kitty had not been so keen, Alison would have put her foot down firmly. Her heart leapt to her mouth now, as she visualized the cheerfully exuberant child up there, suspended crazily between floor and ceiling. For Alison had never trusted this Mr 'Parkinson' Forson (as on occasion he preferred to call himself). Now she despised him as a deceitful liar.

His family home, indeed! The oil king was just another jumped up American come to England to ape his betters – one of the swelling numbers of 'nouveau riche', as Jennifer might say.

The source of the irritating bangs was easily discovered: the door of the first years' classroom. It swung in the draught from that window Miss Prosser had opened to let out the smoke from the infernal man's cigar.

The girl moved across the floor silently, then stuck her head out of the window into the tempest. Leaves and twigs lay everywhere, soaked and flattened against the ground, visible even in that thinnest of beams shed by her torch.

'Queer?' she found herself muttering. 'I was sure the old fleabag left it on the catch.'

The cooling rain battered her face but refreshed her. The gale streamed through her hair. She remained, eyes gratefully closed, within the freedom of the outside world for as long as possible. She wished she could be a small animal, hidden snugly in its sandy burrow under some mighty beech up there on the hill.

But even great trees can fall in such a storm and, with that thought, the girl pulled the casement to. With the wind suddenly excluded, was that a less natural sound that she had heard somewhere behind? She hated to think what she might see, and nervously played her torch around the walls. Nothing. Then it came again. This time there was no mistaking the creak of wooden boards. Someone or something was up there on the haunted landing. Oh, Jiminy!

The very marrow in Alison's bones seemed to have frozen. Her limbs failed to function. She stood petrified. It took minutes, in fact, to relearn even how to move. And when she did, her joints seemed to creak like the stairs up which, a few moments later, she was shining her torch. But then its puny light became unnecessary, for in that second blazed the most vivid flash of lightning yet.

In that brief moment, Alison saw - not the grey lady but, in all its infinite horror - the monk.

As, accompanied by a dreadful clap of thunder right overhead, the thing leaned down its frightful face, she saw a pair of eyeless sockets gazing at her from above black tufts. That wiry hair sprouted from visible cheekbones, through shrivelled and broken dry skin. Only just in time did the girl stuff a hanky in her mouth to stifle the scream that would surely have wakened the whole school.

When she dared, tremulously, to play her torch again over the banisters, the monstrosity itself had gone. But its reason for having been there on the landing remained. For the portrait hung askew; and in a second the girl had bounded up the rest of the stairs. A groping hand must have reached down to thrust the picture aside. Now, heart thumping with excitement, Alison reached up, pushing at the old painting until . . . there it was, there was the place, a space in the wall, as she knew it had to be.

Was she too late, or had the thief been disturbed just in time? In that niche was secreted a small, open, brass-bound box. In that box her probing fingers found – nothing.

Riven by doubt and indecision, the frustrated sleuth remained where she was with a deeply furrowed brow.

Should she have given chase? No. Alison could not be a match for such a villain. Should she, then, arouse Miss Cowley, and Miss Cowley, then, the police? One thing was clear. Miss Prosser had not left that window open to let out smoke.

Gazing into the inscrutable face before her in the torchlight, Alison knew this to be a matter of the utmost delicacy. The authorities pay little heed to 'curses'. Nobody but Teddy would understand how the honour of the Daynes had been violated. It was up to the Daynes to avenge that insult. Teddy would know what to do. The boy was nearly a solicitor, after all. She would telephone his office the very first thing next morning.

What Alison had not bargained for was the fact that even solicitors-to-be are not usually in their offices before nine o'clock. And at nine in schools, lessons are apt to begin. And since the person giving that lesson was Miss Prosser herself, the exhausted girl thought it wise to attend.

She ground out her frustration until break. At least she had established one fact for what it was worth. Miss Prosser was still there, at any rate, unabashed and in a mood that seemed almost benign.

When Alison had been asked how many gallons of water would fit into a barrel three feet by six feet and had replied 'it depends on the shape of the barrel' with considerable hauteur, the mistress's face had actually broken into a smile. It was an unpleasant one, certainly, but a smile nevertheless.

Then at break Anthea Turnbull of the sixth had grabbed Sally to help with the make-up room and Alison to assist the man with the final arrangement of the high wire. Matters of life and death come first. Not until lunchtime had Alison been able to get at the phone. Then it was only to be told that Mr Dayne had gone to Court that day and would not be back until five! Oh, quel horreur! Alison gave up.

'Tell him I'm coming round. If I don't see him at the cottage, I'll sit in the office.'

'All right, all right!' had retorted the crabby voice at the other end, and the phone had slammed back.

Alison decided to have a headache and a lie down during

French. She was just too jumpy, and for the rest of the afternoon there were no more lessons anyway.

All was activity in and around the school hall. Girls arranged chairs neatly in rows, to the strains of the Tannhauser overture. Girls ran back and forth carrying cups of tea and slices of cake to the staff, who hovered about chewing and trying to look superior, but were just as excited as everyone else.

There was an atmosphere of expectancy not usually evident in such minor productions. It was rumoured that Mr Forson had arranged for an impresario from New York to be present at this show, and Verity's voice could be heard above everyone else's directing her 'dressers' down to the last and finest detail.

Alison was having a certain amount of strained argument with Kitty, about how much enthusiasm the young Ariel was expected to inject into her part.

'I should slide very slowly and carefully, if you've got to do it at all. And don't wave your arms about.'

'It's not my arms, it's my wings.'

'Well, your wings, then. Keep tight hold of what you're supposed to hold.'

'I've got to flap my wings, Ali, or I won't look as though I'm a sprite. I shall be in a *sling*. That's the whole idea. I work the wings with my hands as I'm slithering along.'

'Well anyway,' Alison shuddered, 'I might not be here some of the time.'

'Oh, Alison!'

'I've got to go and see brother Teddy – only for a minute.'

'Well, I should jolly well hurry and get back, or you might not see me! It must be *frightfully* important to be dashing off now.'

'What was that?' came Sally's voice from the make-up room. She emerged, her cheeks rouged rather beautifully and her lips succulent with red paint. '*Alison*! You're not going over without *me*? I'm a lost soul hanging around here. Can't I come? I'm so fed up. Should have been in the soppy thing, I s'pose.

'Not this time, actually, Sal . . .'

'Oh, *do* be a sport! We can manage it easily, there and back, before this starts, if we pedal fast. I'll race you.'

'Sally, I do feel an awful heel but I wonder – you wouldn't stay and cover up for me again, just this once? It's so frightfully important.' She drew the other girl aside. 'I'm worried about Kitty, old lovekins, I really am. My nerves are just about as strung up as that wretched wire.'

'More Dayne talk, I suppose. Oh well . . .' Sally sighed. Then a radiant smile broke over her exquisitely pretty face. 'Of course I'll stay, you ass. They want me here, anyway, to help with the make-up. Give the dear thing my love. I'm still waiting to hear what happened to you in the night! You promised to tell, remember.'

'I'll reveal all as soon as I can, never fear.'

The girl looked anxiously at the clock. The minutes had ticked by so slowly. 'I think I'll go now.' She managed a wry smile. 'I *know* Teddy wanted to show you his bike. I might even get him to the play.'

'Oh, Ali!'

Their hands touched, and Alison was gone.

The last time she and Sally had travelled to see Teddy had been on the country bus that idled its way, zigzagging from village to village, through the pleasant landscape. Stout farming ladies had been picked up and deposited, ladies with empty baskets on the way in and full ones on the way back, plus the odd live hen from the market.

On this occasion there was no time for such dawdling. The most direct route from the school was a narrow mossy lane that first skirted the grounds of Coxley Grange and then plunged through thick woods for most of the rest of the way to Stalminster.

Now Alison was cycling furiously along it, her head bent over the handlebars. Everywhere lay evidence of last night's storm. Leaves and twigs littered the lane's damp slippery surface, while the profusion of flowers along the verges were squashed and browbeaten, as though they'd never be able to heave themselves back to life. Jays squabbled in the woods. A sheep leaped over a wall. Two magpies flashed by in front, making her look up from the handlebars. It was lucky she did. Alison drew up with a squeal of brakes.

A large tree had fallen right across the road from bank to bank. Huge roots projected from the sand and flints on one bank, hundreds of branches completely blocked the other. The girl had to waste precious minutes heaving her cycle over the trunk and then waiting on the other side, while she got her breath back.

But then she was on the machine again and pedalling away as if for dear life until, suddenly bursting out of the trees, there lay her goal. The town rose like a ladder almost from her feet.

Stalminster is unique among small southern English towns in that it perches on a hill. Narrow cobbled streets of picturesque cottages wind erratically up to the very top on whose bump sits squarely, as it has done these last six hundred years, the old parish church. In a more lowly position, in the church's shadow, may also be found the office of Toogood and Marshall, Solicitors, and it was towards this place that Alison now painfully laboured.

This last part of the journey was by far the worst. She couldn't very well vow she'd never come again. Under the ramparts and in that same steep street sat Teddy's snug cottage; and beyond the church, the town itself. She called in at number five. No; Edward was not back for his tea yet.

'And don't you go making him late. I got the whist drive tonight . . .'

On an office chair she sat biting her nails for a good twenty minutes before the door finally flew open and in burst . . .

'Teddy!'

'Alison! What's up? Won't be a jiff . . .'

A few moments later, more or less out of uniform and back to his old familiar self, he emerged from the office with Alison in tow.

Up the narrow alleyway they walked, heads bowed already in deep and earnest conversation. Then, as they came out into the High Street, Teddy was seen to throw back his head and laugh.

'I can only tell you that's what the book said!' Alison retorted, as they awaited a chance to cross the road.

'All right; all right,' Teddy replied easily. 'But in your book – you've just mentioned it yourself – the disasters didn't happen until the treasure had actually left the house.' He grabbed hold of his cousin's hand. They crossed to the market. 'As far as I can make out, *you* seem to have been having them pretty consistently since the beginning of term.'

'Don't be more of a goof than you have to be, Teds,' Alison pleaded as they hurried along the pavement. 'They're not the real ones. They only lead up to it. They're not the *cataclysm*, the actual *finish* of St Ursula's as it's always been. That's due to happen any minute now. Where are we going, by the way?'

'Sorry. It won't take a tick. Just got to get a few things before the shops shut. Where were we?' He barged into a confectioner's. 'Oh yes! Then why did Kitty see her amazing grey ghost more than two weeks ago?'

'It can only have been a warning, you see, Teds. The grey lady must have had some idea in her mind, already, of what was going to happen . . .'

A woman in front of them, dressed in a grey fur coat, turned and lifted her eyebrows.

'Kitty must, you mean . . .' said Teddy.

'Must what?'

'. . . have had that premonition. I'll take half a pound of chocolate dragees, two dozen large humbugs and a box of butterscotch, please.' The dentist knew Teddy's sweet tooth. 'She's pretty good at premonitions, our Kitty. Always knows when I want her to run down to the sweet shop.'

Alison herself had hardly noticed the purchase of all these good things.

'Don't fool about,' she said desperately as they emerged

from the shop. 'You're trying to pour cold water again – suggesting she imagined it.'

'I'm not, actually. Anyway, it boils down to the same thing. If the grey lady's our ancestor, presumably she could be working through Kitty's mind.'

'Golly! I'd never thought of that.'

'It's a matter of honour, one way or the other.' Teddy grinned.

'The honour of the Daynes!' echoed Alison, a little thrill going through her as she gazed at her cousin with fervent admiration, 'which adds up to . . .'

''Ere. Buy the young lady a few strawberries, sir. Not a squashy one among 'em.' They were passing the fruit stall.

'Why not.' Teddy dipped his hand into his pocket again.

'. . . which adds up, as I was just saying, to the Honour of the School.'

'Well, I'm no expert, but I'll take your word for it, old bean-bag. And except for the fact that the monk'll be in the next county by now, I should think the place should be jolly grateful having you there at all. It really makes one start thinking about *predestination*. Here, have a strawberry – or two,' he said, stuffing them both in her mouth at once as if to put an end to such sentimental rambling. 'Your dad having the idea of sending you to St Ursula's; then Kitty coming along and seeing the ghost; and that making you read the book.'

'Don't mock, Teds,' Alison gulped as they prepared to cross to Teddy's street again.

'Sorry, dear old golobosh – but isn't it time to revert to reality? As a solicitor-to-be . . .'

'Not that again.'

'. . . as a man with a razor sharp legal mind, the facts as I see them are these. Number one: we don't even know whether there ever was such a 'Talisman' in that box of yours but, assuming there was, then I reckon if the treasure belonged to our ancestor, it must still be ours; and I want it back.'

'Oh Teddy,' Alison cried, stopping and wailing. 'That's

wrong – and entirely irrelevant!'

'It isn't irrelevant. It may be wrong, but it isn't irrelevant.'

'It *is*.' The girl stamped her foot. 'That Talisman belongs to our school. You don't go around pinching furniture out of a house when you've sold it to someone.'

'*Was* the Talisman ever handed over to the school? That old Farquhar idiot probably hasn't even heard of the Daynes, let alone any treasure. No, I'm going to start an enquiry.'

'Oh please don't go spilling the beans to all and sundry, Teds. I couldn't bear embarrassing family rot to spread round the school just now . . . not on top of everything else. As it is, Sally thinks I'm a stuck up sneak.'

'Does she? I'll give the silly ass a quick whizz on the Thunderer. That'll change her tune.'

'And Prosey's got eyes like a hawk. She'll soon get the idea that something's afoot.'

'Provided she's not in jail – leaving the window deliberately open like that. It's monstrous.'

'I can't be certain,' replied Alison slowly as they emerged out on to the top of the hill, 'but I reckon the thief must have climbed through just before I came into the room. Otherwise, he'd have had time to put the window on the catch again.'

Even the cynical Teddy was really listening now.

'Hovering around the room, all the time you were there? Feller sounds like a professional.'

'The picture *was* skew whiff . . .'

'Exactly. And the box empty. All of which goes to make your Miss Prosser an accomplice after the fact, if not actually a thief herself. But, I mean, just supposing we're both absolutely wrong about this?'

'You *mean*,' corrected Alison dismally, 'there's no proof . . .'

'I'm only trying to protect you, old thing. You know what they'd say.'

'That I was trying to get my revenge for what she did to me last year?'

'I can just see it in the papers. "Chaos at exclusive girls' boarding school, as pupil accuses second mistress." Might even make the Nationals.'

'Oh, please don't go on . . .'

'No, really – the thing's potential dynamite. Stealing the Dayne family heritage, by Gad! Will this woman stop at nothing?'

Alison sank on to a seat.

From here the whole of the county spread away in a patchwork of fields and woods. Somewhere unseen in that pleasant land lay St Ursula's School for Girls. She had tried hard to protect it. Now it seemed that the school was finally doomed, never to be the same again. With this latest diatribe from Teddy, all hope had fizzled away. A small figure could be seen half way down the hill, arms akimbo.

'Miss Alison, Mr Teddy, sir!' came the faint voice.

It was Mrs Trimble. They caught up.

'Mrs Trimble . . .'

'Oh, Mr Teddy, sir. I've been waiting for you all day, that I have.' She wiped her eye with a corner of her apron. 'I got some news.'

'What is it, Mrs Trimble?'

'Well sir, listen. My George has been keeping his ear pretty much to the ground over at Coxley's since what I tell 'im about your little sister and that monk. 'Twas only this morning, hoeing down the drive, 'ee 'ear voices behind the rhododendrons – a man and a woman they was, 'bout eleven o'clock, and talking about your school, and some plan they'd made for last night goin' all wrong . . .'

'How did it go wrong?'

'Well the man 'ee reckon 'ee *been* to the school all right and, least ways so far as George could make out, got what 'ee wanted. But then you'll never believe this – in a flash of lightning 'ee reckon he see the old Semley spook – that beautiful young woman I was tellin' you 'bout what's got the picture 'anging on the wall above the main stairs. Must 'ave been 'is guilty conscience, we reckon.' Mrs Trimble laughed throatily. 'Wasn't it a terrible storm? They do say Buzzybee Bottom flooded good and proper, and trees down and all.'

'Good Heavens.'

'Good 'eavens is right. She must of come to get her vengeance on that dratted, thieving beggar. I got my suspicions . . .'

'Is that all?'

While Alison listened open mouthed, a slow grin had crossed Teddy's face. He had to stop himself laughing out loud, for what the 'monk' had seen, of course, had been Alison!

'Oh no, sir – not by a long chalk; because in his state of shock the chap – whoever 'twas – dropped whatever 'twas that ee'd gone to get, and now they've arranged for another do tonight! Tell you the truth, the woman said she'd done her bit of the bargain by opening some winder and was tryin' to stop 'im going again, but the bloke wasn't having any. He said 'ee'd get what he left behind and then scare all the girls stupid while they was in some play they're putting on over there . . .'

'*The Tempest!*' Alison gasped. 'Oh glory – with Kitty on the high wire!'

'He did his best, did George, trying to see who 'twas; but ee's a slow sorta chap, is my 'usband, and them bushes are so darn thick you can't see nothing, only twigs. Now, 'ave I done any good, because they do say St Ursula's is in real danger now.'

'Any *good*? I should say you have, Mrs Trimble! You've been an utter brick; and here's a shilling for your trouble.'

'Oh lor, no sir, nothing like that. George wouldn't want it, either.'

Alison, biting her lip, had glanced at the old church clock.

'Teddy, I've *got* to get back. The rehearsal must be starting any minute – if it's not already begun.'

'All right. You stay there. Leave your bike. I'll get the Thunderer.'

'That's what comes,' Mrs Trimble sagely observed, 'of

lettin' all and sundry into your grounds. Them village lads, they're a proper show off. I don't know what things are coming to these days, I don't really.'

Teddy had already wheeled out the big bike and was preparing himself for travel. First he buttoned on his helmet; then his long leather coat. He handed Alison a pair of goggles. She fitted them round the hood of her mac.

'Hurry, Teddy!'

'Come on! Climb aboard.'

A kick from the starter, and with a mighty blast the machine leapt to life.

'Goodbye, goodbye, Mrs Trimble. If there's anything we can do in return . . .'

'Get along with you; and the best of luck!'

The machine rolled down the hill. Alison turned and, delving in her mac, let fly her hanky. The plump country lady waved, then disappeared round the corner.

And now they were out in open country. As Verity Lamton swam fishlike under the brilliant arc lights of fame in green clinging velvet, the rescuers of the school, heads bent to the task, were eating up the miles which Alison had, by contrast, so doggedly laboured over just a couple of hours before.

> '"If by your art, my dearest father, you have
> Put the wild waters in this roar, allay them.
> The sky, it seems, would pour down stinking pitch,
> But that the sea, mounting to th' welkin's cheek,
> Dashes the fire out."'

Unknowingly about to be lifted out of that sea of craning eager faces and plunged back into real life, Miranda meanwhile unleashed on mighty Prospero her suplicating girlish charm and guile.

'"O! I have suffer'd
With those that I saw suffer: a brave vessel,
Who had, no doubt, some noble creatures in her,
Dash'd all to pieces."'

The audience wished to see. Because the front row was entirely occupied by adults, they found it difficult. Some had begun to stand on their seats. Mr Forson was there, with or without his theatrical friend – who knew? Major Farquhar had already dropped off to sleep while Miss Cowley, transported for a liquid moment into sheer pleasure, licked her lips and listened. Miss Prosser's eyes were bright for a different reason, while all the other members of staff nodded and gazed in approval, ignorant of what was soon to befall.

'"Here cease more questions."' The bearded magician had spoken. Prospero leaned quietly over his obediently yielding charge.

'"Thou art inclin'd to sleep. 'Tis a good dullness,
And give it away; I know thou canst not choose . . ."'

The motor bike squealed in the damp leaves and skidded to a halt.

'Oh scissors!' Alison yelled. 'I'd forgotten the fallen tree. We'll have to go all the way back.'

'No, cling on,' ordered Teddy curtly, coming to a snap decision. 'We'll go by Coxley's – through the woods and past the lake.'

As Verity closed her eyes and, with a gasp, sank back into the cushions laid there by herself specifically for that purpose, Prospero lifted his arms and called out:

'"Come away, servant, come! I am ready now.
Approach, my Ariel; come!'"

Enter Kitty Dayne, on the balcony. Her wings are yellow, in

place, and ready to flap obediently. She is already clipped to the flying harness. She bestows on the audience one of her most beaming smiles.

> '"All hail great master! grave sir, hail! I come
> To answer thy best pleasure; be't to fly,
> To swim, to dive into the fire, to ride
> On the curl'd clouds: to thy strong bidding task
> Ariel and all his quality."'

But what is this? In addition to the sprite, the master seems to have called up another and far less cheering shade. At that moment, unaccountably, the audience began to scream. A looming grey shape had appeared behind the child. Being at the rear of the balcony, however, the apparition's sickening face was visible only to those at the back of the hall. A couple of small girls fainted. The adults turned round in sudden annoyance.

Kitty, too, frowned. Whatever was the matter with them? Peering down into the darkness, she tried to fathom why they were leaping about and shouting so. Then she came to a happy conclusion. They were, of course, clamouring for her, head over heels about her performance! It was a bit early; but naturally they could recognize real talent when they saw it. She prepared to continue. The monk advanced. The audience watched, entranced, as the performer (who featured in no set book *they* knew) lifted its bony arms – then . . .

'Look out! Look out!' they screeched. 'Kitty . . . just look behind you! It's the ghost!'

The child turned. The ghastly skull was peering right into her face, the bony fingers stretched out to grasp her throat. She uttered a piercing scream, then took off down the high wire. Immediately, the lights went out.

The motor bike, meanwhile, was racing out of the woods and along the side of the lake. How melancholy and deserted the scene now looked, the long graceful bridge on which the performances would have taken place splayed out in a cold evening mist.

All had been peace there till the bike's powerful thunder rent the tranquil scene. Ducks raced head first in protest over the erstwhile mirror surface of the water. As the machine bounced into the air then thumped down on to the bridge itself, the planks beneath its wheels rattled out a startled tattoo.

Only a few more hundred yards to go. Down the long drive they raced, and out into the road along which, of late, one could usually see at least two or three groups of chattering girls on their way over to Coxley Grange. Tonight, there was no-one. *They* were all inside, in a scene where bedlam reigned.

The lights had still not come on. Torches flashed, while people tripped over one another in the darkness in a vain effort to scramble to the doors.

The Thunderer blasted over the last stretch. And as it shot past the green St Ursula's paddocks Alison, looking away over Teddy's shoulder towards the entrance, suddenly yelled in his ear:

'Stop Teddy, stop! It's the monk! Quickly, before he hears us.'

The engine died. Quietly, the big bike slid into the hedge.

For a moment they peered together over the bank. A curious gangling figure, immensely tall and thin, could be seen struggling across the expanse of lawn. It was heading for the school chapel. Teddy jumped from his seat.

'I'll get the blighter. Now, you just do exactly as I say.'

The interior of the school chapel was never a comfortable place. Even on Sunday evenings, when so many young voices were lifted in song, the chill barely lifted. Their breath would hang on the raw air like ever thickening fog.

Now, in the deathly silence of the evening, a sour light filtered in through the great yew. Leaving the heavy oak door open behind her Alison, with slow tread, tried to walk steadily down the aisle. Everything in that place seemed to be watching and listening. A few birds twittered outside the lanceolate windows. A small animal ran back into a chink in the wall. When something creaked behind that mouldering screen of carved oak, she resisted the temptation to look back.

She had entered as though in complete innocence. While she held her breath now, someone was trying to creep soundlessly round behind her. She felt his touch, almost, on the nape of her neck as he passed within a whisker. In a second he was away and out of the building, someone running full tilt, straight into the flying, crashing shoulders of wing three-quarter Edward Dayne.

There came a thud and a gasp. The tall, swaying thing of grey cloth hung in the air, for a moment crazily suspended. When it toppled, amidst a jangle of spewed out clocks, the skull parted company with those whirling shrouds and spun away, still grinning, across the slippery grass.

Teddy was fighting something and nothing. What rolled out of a turmoil of erstwhile immensely tall monkish robes was of course – well . . . the last thing either of them, in the circumstances, could have expected to see, a tiny person no more than four feet tall.

As the dwarf sprang with monkey-like agility to his own full height, there came another ruthless thud and down he went again; struggling like a wild thing with a cursing tongue and quite demoniacal glare. Evidently, Teddy did not like that facial language, and proceeded to rub it away into Mr Brisling's turf. Locked in combat, they rolled together back and forth.

Alison dodged in and out of the fighting pair, trying to get at another object that in the melee had fallen from the small man's jacket. She pounced, and grabbed the smooth green, glinting pendant stone with its falling chain, gazed in wonder only for a moment, then slipped the precious treasure into her pocket.

She clutched it there, the future of the school at last within her grasp.

Teddy hauled his victim to his feet. His fist went back.

'Spill the beans, fathead.'

'Mister – I've already spilled 'em.'

'Enough of your wisecracks. Just get on with the details.'

'All right, all right, I'll talk if you just let me breathe.'

Five minutes later, an unexpected trio crashed through the old front portal of St Ursula's School for Girls. The lights were fully on again: arc lights, spot lights, every sort of light, blazing away on that scene of confusion.

'Make way! Make way! Here's your monk.'

'What the thump? Well, I'll be jiggered. It's the gypsy – and he *is* a dwarf. I told you he was a dwarf.'

'Is Kitty all right?' Alison forced her way through the scrum to grab Sally's shoulder. The girl spun round.

'Eh? Oh, fit as a fiddle, old fruit,' she beamed. 'It's St Ursula's that's in danger.'

'What?'

'Mind your backs, everyone. Clear a path.'

Sally's reply was drowned in the thrilled approval of the girls who swarmed round Teddy and his sullen victim, trying to catch a glimpse of this legendary midget.

'*Our* monk? That little tadpole? Somebody else's, maybe – but no; not ours!'

Kitty, who was being fanned as she sat with eyelids closed, now speedily opened one. She ran, sucking her thumb, and buried herself in her cousin's comforting presence.

'What was it you were trying to say?' yelled Alison, and Sally glanced hopelessly over her shoulder.

'Only that you've arrived not a moment too soon, old grappler! They're in that study now signing the old school away.'

'*What?*'

In the comparative silence of Miss Devine's elegant retreat, Major Farquhar sat with his eyes running up and down the impressive document that lay on the desk before him, for a last, nervous check.

Although there were, of course, no further questions he could think of, a person could never be too sure, and his hand still twitched over the pen.

It was a very sudden and momentous decision for any single individual to have to take. Yet the rest of the Governors had been most pressing, and during the last twenty-four hours the document had been studied in exhaustive detail.

There could be no last minute hitches, surely? The presence of Miss Prosser behind him unnerved the Major. He wished she would not stand so close, so motionless and erect, like that wraith of hers which had appeared, as if to order, up there on the balcony a few minutes earlier. The military man did not care to be rushed. In war, nevertheless, one *had* to be decisive.

'You're sure you wouldn't like another hour or two?' the woman was enquiring irritably, as if divining his thoughts.

Indeed, it was all *she* could do to keep that mask of serene calmness clamped in position. With her goal so nearly within her grasp, she knew she should not be suggesting anything of the sort. She should have been hissing, 'Get on with it you old fool!' not handing over even more time.

With Miss Cowley a shrivelled heap on the sofa and Farquhar still trying to gasp out a reply, Miss Prosser knew she had already given far too much. Curiously even for Mr Forson, it seemed, the moment had come perhaps a little too quickly, and heaven knows, *he'd* had enough chance to consider. He'd engineered the whole idea of the exchange, and yet . . .

And yet, as the American gazed with such intensity out across the pristine smoothness of the St Ursula's lawns, how fiercely he clutched that cigar. Oh, would the old fool *never* stop dithering? The second mistress felt about to expire. At last! It appeared the moment had arrived.

'No. I don't think so, Miss Prosser.' The Major spoke crisply. 'Now. You want my signature.' The pen lifted. It sank a little; then it rose again. It was hovering.

Oh, could not those terrible children be quiet? Miss

Prosser's gimlet eyes wished they could bore through wood. Did they not know the dramatic importance of this moment?

Now, as Teddy had almost reached that barrier which divided those two worlds, the row reached frenetic proportions and the Major looked up enquiringly.

No! The mistress was again drawing in her breath. She could hardly believe this delay. Even as, unable to resist the overwhelming provocation any longer, her mouth opened for the yell that would have awakened at least six packs of nearby hounds, the Chairman had in his own mind reached his decision. The pen had fallen – finally. As it touched paper, there came a thump and a bang. Then *everyone* looked up. The door had burst open.

'Don't sign, Major!'

'What?' shrieked Prosser, in utter disbelief and dismay. For there, in the firm grasp of this interfering young busybody, was her own much despised accomplice. 'What,' she yelped, 'is the meaning of this intrusion?'

Teddy was quite happy to oblige with the answer to that particular question. As Miss Cowley sat up, the boy thrust forward his prisoner. His voice quivered.

'I'll tell you the meaning, madam. It's quite simple. *This* is your ghost. He's confessed to *everything*.'

'Good Heavens!' the Major cried in amazement, as the pen fell from his hand and the cigar from Mr Forson's mouth.

'And as a man of the law,' Teddy continued calmly, 'I must say I've never heard a more disgraceful story.' He turned in indignation to Mr Forson. 'You, sir. What do you mean by frightening little children out of their wits? And why, indeed? Simply to line your pockets with a few extra million quid. Don't you have enough already?'

'Is this true?' Pop-eyed with disbelief, Major Farquhar turned to the American and almost begged, 'Deny it sir . . . Deny it!'

'I can't, Major.' The American, finding his voice for the first time in the last ten minutes, shook his head ruefully.

'Some you win,' he sighed. 'Some you lose . . .'

'Well, I must say, it baffles me . . .'

Hand quivering, the ex-military genius reached for his hanky.

'Coal, Major,' Teddy explained patiently. 'You know – black diamonds. I took the liberty of making a few private investigations, and it seems there's enough of the stuff under this floor to toast every crumpet in Christendom.'

'You can't mean,' the man exploded at last, like one of his own grenades, 'that he meant to knock the old place down?'

'Seems like it, sir,' Teddy confirmed cheerfully. 'He'd tried to buy the school from Miss Devine, but of course she wouldn't hear of it. Thought the feller was cuckoo. But then, of course, she was called away to Bosnavia.'

'And when the cat's away – the mice'll play, eh?'

Mr Forson received a withering glare. If looks could kill, that gentleman should have shrivelled away. Actually, the American showed no sign of doing so. He'd attended worse board meetings than this. No, there was something else boring into that sensitive flesh, something he'd been unsuccessfully trying to put into words ever since he'd suggested to Kitty and that little witch, Nesta Roberts, his idea about the play.

Teddy was now answering the Major's observation with considerable care.

'Exactly. Kitty's grey lady gave him just the clue he needed.' And while the boy's mind struggled to choose the right succinct words, so Alison grappled with something far less tangible – something completely *outside* reason. She had been awaiting her opportunity to perform a sacred task. Now, as the crowd drifted momentarily from the region of the main staircase, she left Kitty for a moment.

'If he could exploit the ghost business,' Teddy slowly went on as Alison mounted the stairs, 'arrange a few extra hauntings and make 'em shockers into the bargain . . . then, with St Ursula's in chaos, all he'd have to do would be step in with the offer.'

'And we'd jump at it! Well, I'm blessed!'

'In fact, everything was going like ninepence.'

'And then,' came Miss Cowley's sonorous voice as she rose unexpectedly from the couch, 'Miss Prosser took charge.'

Quivering with indignation, the acting Headmistress wagged the finger of scorn at that culprit, trapped behind the Major's desk.

'I knew nothing about it!' the second mistress retorted, red as fire, her mask of inscrutability broken at last.

'You most certainly did after you had made the suggestion about the new St Ursula's at your dinner with Mr Forson, madam. So do not deny it. Oh yes,' the angry accuser went on mercilessly, 'I am well aware how much you always resented Miss Devine, thinking you should have been chosen Headmistress in her stead!' Miss Cowley paused, her chest heaving. 'Coming to me, apologizing, as if butter would not melt in your mouth. The very thought! I confess, at the time, I was so relieved I quite forgot even to *wonder* whether there might be an ulterior motive. What were you going to call your new school? Prosser's Prison? Ha! And I should hold on to *that* little weasel, if I were you,' she declared roundly, nodding at the dwarf. Teddy, it must be admitted, had relaxed his hold on the tiny man. 'He and Miss Prosser were in league all the time. I saw them, talking in the woods.

'You will regret this slander, madam,' Prosser screeched in return.

Then something happened.

For a moment the background seemed to become blurred. A mist appeared to pass before their transfixed eyes. With a small chink, the Talisman and chain had been returned to their proper place in the wall, hopefully for another hundred years of undisturbed peace.

The mist cleared again. With everyone back in motion, Mr Forson's voice was raised in sudden and unexpected dissent.

'Oh no she won't, you old fleabag,' he shouted now, with some conviction.

The door into the hall slammed open. The throng of girls divided to allow Prosey's passage as, quivering with rage and humiliation, the second mistress strode forth.

A tremendous gale of laughter swept through the building at that moment. It was felt from the dizzy heights of the sixth, right down to that very smallest girl who had blown the bosun's whistle. Miss Prosser made her exit, hopefully for ever.

Waggling his cigar in the study doorway, the American swelled with indignation at his own inexcusable foolishness.

'No-one's going to regret anything any more,' he bawled. 'I'll see to that!'

Evidently taking him at his word, the small and agile ex-circus performer seized his moment at last and, wriggling from Teddy's grasp, darted across the room. In a trice, he had thrust up the sash window and with a flying leap sailed through the open space, straight into a pair of open, welcoming arms. They were the longest arms of all, unfortunately for him: those of the English law.

Clad now sombrely in his pinstripe suit of office, the bogus surveyor received the flying missile with a glad but sobering cry.

'Not so fast, sonny Jim,' he warned; and, holding his struggling catch at arm's length, he looked slowly up to the gaping faces in the window. 'As you see,' he explained patiently, as if to a crowd of baboons, 'I am a surveyor in more ways than one. Now, young feller-me-lad, there are one or two questions I'd like to ask you down at the station.' In final salute, he touched his bowler hat; then, 'Evening, all!' he bid them, turning on his heel. It was a difficult enough feat in a flower bed, but he managed it, and then portentously strode away.

'Pinch me, someone,' Miss Cowley sighed, flopping back once more on to the sofa. 'I can't believe all this is happening.'

The Major approached her humbly.

'Miss Cowley, I feel I owe you an apology . . .'

'Oh . . . think nothing of it, Major Farquhar. This kind of thing, I'm afraid, happens to me all the time.'

'Well, in that case,' responded the Major equably, 'that's all right then. Now, Forson. An explanation, if you please.'

'OK, OK. You're right, sir, you deserve it. So I admit an error of judgement; yet I swear that long before your crazy Prosser dame forced that meeting on us yesterday, I'd made up my mind to forget the whole darn business.' The American turned back, waving his cigar the way she had gone. 'Never could stand that woman's face. I mean, listen, Major – all I wanted was a straight swap between friends. There's nothing so bad in that, is there? I thought, they'll still have a school but a much *better* one. Now,' he declared devoutly, 'I see I was wrong. This crummy old building means much more to all of you guys here than it ever could to me.'

He was wandering out into the hall again – a sad scene of a play cut off in its prime – and everyone followed, as people always followed Mr Forson.

'I mean, *look* at it.' The American waved his arm expansively and everyone looked. (He'd have made quite a good school teacher, Alison thought, rejoining a lonely Sally on a chair in the back row of the stalls.) '*I* started all this. Why should I want to spoil it now? The coal was never the real reason, I swear. I promise you, I'd told the gypsy guy to lay off his tricks, I don't know *how* long ago. But you know what these little squirts are. He'd gotten carried away by his acting role, plus a little thieving on the side, I guess. Anyways . . .' and here Mr Forson looked down at the various heads which by now seemed to have gathered sociably under his arms '. . . the kids were never really frightened. They enjoy ghosts. They lap 'em up – isn't that right, kids?'

'We do rather, sometimes,' a small child in costume admitted. 'Priscilla said she wanted to dress as one, actually, and come on during the rehearsal as a jape!'

A ripple of easy laughter passed through the assembled throng.

'I didn't!' replied the object of mirth, red as fire.

'Yes you did, you fibber! But the gypsy did it an awful lot better.'

'You see,' offered Mr Forson, 'it's a kinda thrill for everyone, ain't it? Major, life's too short to start taking anything seriously.'

'Oh, don't be horrid to Mr Forson,' Nesta begged, looking up into that wicked old face. 'We like him so much, and he likes us, I know he does. He only wanted to be Lord of the Manor – like my father is at home.'

As Miss Cowley and the military man looked at each other, the American cleared his throat.

'Yes, I guess I did.'

This devout admission was made after a suitably rueful pause. Yet it was only another of his roles in the great drama of life, Miss Cowley supposed. All the world was a stage to him; and all the men and women merely players.

'Then he should have stayed where he was,' the Major grumbled fretfully. 'The house of the Forsons – the Parkinson branch at any rate – stood where Coxley Grange is now. Burnt down in 1703.'

For the first time, the American *really* lost his cool.

'You mean,' he gaped, 'we never lived at Semley here at *all*?'

'Good Heavens, no!' laughed his informant in a voice like a stone crusher's. 'This was built as a dower house for the fifth marchioness in 1544, when her husband – a chap called Dale or Dayne or something – died.' Alison rose like a jack-in-the-box from her seat at the back of the hall, then flopped back again out of sight. 'In fact, it's her portrait up there on the stairs.'

'Oh dear.' Teddy had joined his unhappy cousin. 'Can this mean . . . ?'

'Go on, rub it in. We're related . . .'

'What?' hooted Sally.

'You never spat it out before, you old sly boots!' Mr Forson yelped.

The Major blew his nose. He'd had the handkerchief at the ready ever since the gypsy had jumped out of the window.

'You never asked. But that's how it was, I assure you.'

'Then that,' decided the millionaire with overwhelming finality, 'is the way I want it to stay.' Was this going to be another of his 'good ideas'? Followed like the Pied Piper by his unabashed admirers, Mr Forson marched out into the porch.

'I guess I've gotten kinda mesmerised by your English girls' school caper,' he admitted to everyone; 'and to make amends, therefore, I'm going to show everybody here today what money *really* means to A. J. Parkinson-Forson.'

'Come on, we must hear *this*,' said Teddy.

'Miss Cowley: money is there to be spent.' Now, it seemed, mistresses, prefects, mariners, sprites – the whole school – were crowding outside in a great tidal wave of expectation. 'So I'm going to spend it. I'm going to mend that leaky old roof of yours, and get the place back to such cracking shape that Miss Devine won't know it from Buckingham Palace. I want to have your darn play put on properly, with marquees down by the lake – and be hanged to your English weather. I want . . .'

'The swimming pool?' piped up someone.

'Yea, that's it. I want a swimming pool bigger and better than the one in the President's own back garden.'

'Oh, Mr Forson!' Miss Cowley sighed, quite dazzled by such largesse. Should she perhaps, after all, remain in teaching, and give up the fruit farm idea altogether? Yes. She really thought that she might.

'Nobody seems to be bothering to thank you two,' said Sally, gazing in the most envious admiration at the incorruptible Daynes. 'Oh, I know I've been fairly frightful these last couple of weeks, Ali. It's just – I can't get Jen off my mind.'

'Brummm, brummm . . .' murmured Alison, in a quiet but fair imitation of the Thunderer.

'Oh yes! Now . . . gosh Sally! Don't you find the air a trifle oppressive out here?'

'Not particularly,' replied that listless sylph of the Remove.

'Well *I* certainly do. How do you fancy a spin on the old pillion?'

For a second the girl stared at this amazing man in utter disbelief and incredulity. How could he have know it was *just* what, at that moment, was needed? Then her face melted.

'Oh Teddy,' she sighed, 'if you really mean it.'

'Well of course I mean it, old down-in-the-dumps.'

'Then in that case,' she cried joyfully, 'I can't think of anything I'd adore quite so much!'

But it was at this moment that the taxi turned and rumbled down the drive of a reprieved St Ursula's School for Girls. In its back seat sat a lonely bandaged figure. The vehicle circled once and then, with a scrunch of brakes, stopped dead. A hand was placed on a doorhandle, the door opened, then out stepped . . .

'Jennifer!'

Sally uttered the glad cry with a happiness that only comes from overwhelming relief. So, suddenly abandoned, Teddy shrugged back at Alison who had just become aware of a damp, sticky hand. It was a *restraining* hand that she could not deny.

'What's up, silly Kitty?' she enquired, bending down solicitously to the worried looking child.

'I don't know, Ali, but I've got ever such a funny feeling in my tummy.'

'D'you want nurse?'

'No, no. I want you to come back inside.'

'Oh dear – why? I'd ever so much like to talk to Jen.'

'No, Ali; this is important, please.'

'Oh, very well.'

The girl allowed her small, anxious charge to lead her back into the now completely abandoned hall.

'Well?'

'Oh, *do* come on,' the child urged desperately, dragging her cousin towards the main stairs. They mounted them together, Alison treading the creaking steps with an unaccountable hesitancy and trepidation. Then both stopped together.

Something *was* there – moving, rustling, *shivering* towards them along the gallery above the stage. Suddenly, it was in their midst. An intangible, all consuming presence wrapped inextricably around them both.

And with the sweetest, the most yearningly tender expression Alison had ever seen on anyone's face before, the grey lady bestowed on them one last regretful, fleeting smile before vanishing before their eyes.

For a long moment two small figures waited there, hand in hand. Then Kitty looked up.

'Is St Ursula's safe now, Ali?'

Alison nodded. She was unable to reply, the tears were welling so. They turned and walked slowly, together, back down the stairs. Outside, a blackbird broke again into cheerful lusty song . . .

Fiction from Granada in paperback.

Holly Hobbie Richard Dubleman £1.25 ☐
The exciting adventures of Liz Dutton who, with her magical friend Holly Hobbie, wrestles with the dangers of the Guatemalan jungle to save her father.

Ivory City Marcus Crouch 95p ☐
A collection of Indian folk tales.

The Trumpeter of Krakov Agnes Szudek 85p ☐
A collection of Polish folk tales.

War of the Computers Granville Wilson 85p ☐
A.D. 2010 and a global war breaks out between the computers which govern Earth.
The Terror Cubes 85p ☐
A.D. 2050 and renegade robots threaten to take over Mankind's society.

Trebizon Series Anne Digby
First Term at Trebizon 85p ☐
Second Term at Trebizon 95p ☐
Summer Term at Trebizon 85p ☐
Boy Trouble at Trebizon 95p ☐
More Trouble at Trebizon 85p ☐
The Tennis Term at Trebizon 85p ☐
Summer Camp at Trebizon 95p ☐
Into the Fourth at Trebizon 95p ☐
An exciting new modern school series about Rebecca Mason and her five friends at boarding school.

The Big Swim of the Summer Anne Digby 60p ☐
Sara seems all set to win the big swimming race until she gets involved with the strange new girl at Hocking School.

Bambi's Children Part One Felix Salten 60p ☐
Bambi's Children Part Two 60p ☐
Fifteen Rabbits 65p ☐
Three books of classic and much loved animal stories.

Shadows in the Pit Robin Chambers 70p ☐
A tense and exciting science fiction adventure.

D881